NEW YORK TIMES BESTSELLING AUTHOR
DEBORAH BLADON

FIRST ORIGINAL EDITION, AUGUST 2017

Copyright © 2017 by Deborah Bladon

All rights reserved. No parts of this book may be reproduced in any form or by any means without written consent from the author.

This is a work of fiction. Names, characters, places and incidents either are the product of the author's imagination or are used factiously. Any resemblance to actual person's, living or dead, events, or locales are entirely coincidental.

ISBN-13: 978-1975740443
ISBN-10: 1975740440
eBook ISBN: 978-1-926440-46-0

Book & cover design by Wolf & Eagle Media

www.deborahbladon.com

Also by Deborah Bladon

THE OBSESSED SERIES
THE EXPOSED SERIES
THE PULSE SERIES
THE VAIN SERIES
THE RUIN SERIES
IMPULSE
SOLO
THE GONE SERIES
FUSE
THE TRACE SERIES
CHANCE
THE EMBER SERIES
THE RISE SERIES
HAZE
SHIVER
TORN
THE HEAT SERIES
MELT
THE TENSE DUET

Chapter 1

Brynn

"It wasn't your virginity that he stole, was it?"

I glance over at my roommate, Sydney Tate, to find her smirking. She's still working her ass off on the elliptical machine she's been on for the past thirty minutes. You'd never know it by looking at her. Not one light brown hair on her head is out of place. I wish I could say the same for my shoulder length black hair. It's twisted up in a messy bun, but it's not helping to cool me off.

Not only did I just spend the better part of thirty minutes on a treadmill, but Smith Booth, asshole extraordinaire and all around man I love to hate arrived right when I hit my stride.

Seeing him here, in my favorite gym, was enough to break my pace. I almost fell off the treadmill mid-jog. I didn't though. I slowed to a walk, checked my pulse and resisted the urge to look in his direction.

Sydney gave in and stared at the man doing reps on the bench press. She wasn't the only one who interrupted their workout to gawk at him.

Smith, in all his black haired, brown eyed, muscular glory, turns heads wherever he goes. A big part of that is the fact that he has one of the most recognizable faces in all of New York City. It's also one of the best looking. I'd never admit that to another soul, but Smith is gorgeous. The problem is he knows it.

Since landing the job as the newest co-host of the most watched morning show in the country, Smith's picture has popped up on every digital billboard in this city. He's quickly become the most sought after single man in Manhattan.

"No one stole my virginity." I run my fingertips over the back of my neck as I step closer to the elliptical. "I gave it willingly to a man I thought I'd marry."

"Cue the violins and flying doves." Sydney presses the palm of her left hand to the middle of her chest. "I think my heart is about to explode."

"Shut up," I joke before I crack open the lid of a bottle of chilled water.

"Obviously, the getting married to your first didn't work out." She nods at my left hand. "There's no ring and you haven't been laid in three months."

Her words hit harder than intended. She has no clue. She doesn't know any details about my life before she moved in with me six months ago. "Remind me again why we are friends, Syd. I confide my sexual secrets in you just to have you throw them back in my face."

"Is Smith Booth one of your sexual secrets?" She exhales deeply as the machine comes to a stop. "Do you hate him so much because he sucks in bed? Did he take and not give? Is that what this is about?"

"I've never slept with him," I answer easily, tugging at the bottom hem of the blue tank I'm wearing. I paired it with an old pair of black yoga pants. It's one of my go-to outfits when I hit the gym. I'm not here to impress anyone. My too-round ass is the reason I drag myself down here three times a week. "He's my brother's friend. Julian and Smith have known each other forever."

I take a long sip of water as I wait for the inevitable remark about what she wants to do with my brother. She's only met him once, but that was enough to fuel her dreams for the past four months.

Muting the comments that my friends have made about Julian over the years has become easy. I don't see what they see when they look at him. I see a supportive, ambitious man who resembles a younger version of our father. We both have black hair and blue eyes, but Julian's face is all hard lines etched to symmetrical perfection. My nose is softer, my chin rounder and my smile is just like my mom's, a little lopsided.

Sydney judges Julian by his polished presence. To her, and most of my single friends, he's my hot older brother. To me, he's the person who encourages me to follow my dreams, and now, he's my silent business partner.

When your surname is Bishop and you live on this island, you can expect someone to ask you at least once a day if you know Julian Bishop, CEO of Bishop Hotels or Fulton Bishop, real estate wizard. My dad owns one of the premier real estate brokerage firms in the state. Bishop and Associates sold more residential properties in New York City last year than any other company.

I'm learning how to master the art of flipping the conversation, so the focus is on me whenever anyone brings up my brother or my dad. It's a constant work in progress.

That's all going to change once my interior design business takes off.

"I haven't forgotten that you told me that Smith stole something from you." Sydney steps down from the machine. "You've never told me what it was. Spit it out. Tell me what he took from you."

I know she's expecting me to say it's my heart or the promise of a happy future, but that's not what this is about.

In my family, there's one tangible thing that you value more than almost anything else.

"It happened three years ago."

"When you were twenty-two?" She lowers her voice and leans in closer. "You've never struck me as the type to stay mad at someone for more than a day. Remind me never to piss you off."

I bite back a grin, squaring my shoulders. "I'm not that type. It's different with Smith. He infuriates me."

"You don't have to tell me. I'm pretty sure I saw a voodoo doll in your bedroom with a picture of his face taped to it."

I look down at the floor with a huff of laughter. "You know that's not true."

"It's just a matter of time until you get one. If looks could kill, Smith would be a goner." She reaches for my hand. "You know you can tell me anything. Give me the goods on Mr. Booth, so I have justification for going over there and kicking his ass."

Sydney is six inches shorter than me, and I'm five foot eight. Smith has a solid foot on her and at least one hundred pounds. I have no doubt she could knock him on his ass just by looking at him. She's beautiful, and from what I can remember, she's exactly his type.

"It's simple." I glance over my shoulder to where Smith is standing next to a woman with red hair. He's even better looking than I remember and he knows it, the bastard. He's playing the part of Prince Charming to a tee, right down to the grin and cock of his dark brow as the woman he's with laughs at something he says. Her eyes move over his bare chest and tight abs to the black shorts he's wearing.

"Brynn." Sydney taps my hand. "Tell me."

I turn back to look at her. "Smith stole the one thing from me that every single woman in Manhattan wants."

It takes a few seconds for her to sit on that and think it through. "A rent controlled apartment with a view of the park?"

I nod slowly, taking pleasure in the fact that all of my well-intentioned lectures have paid off. Sydney is finally learning that owning a piece of the property pie in Manhattan is a better investment than a long term relationship with any man. A diamond engagement ring may seem like the brass ring to many of the women in this city, but an address in the right neighborhood isn't going to break your heart. "Close. Smith Booth stole a brownstone on the Upper East Side that I was desperate to buy. He took it right out of the palm of my hand."

"You're a Bishop," she points out. "Your dad practically runs the New York real estate market.

How the hell did Smith manage to get his hands on a property you wanted?"

"He convinced the seller to take his offer even though it was lower than mine." I shake my head still regretting the fact that I didn't go straight to my dad to help me broker the deal. I used an agent who was a friend of a friend instead. That's what I get for trying to surprise my family. "My terms were better. My offer was the right choice."

"So what happened?" She raises an eyebrow. "What did he offer that you didn't?"

"His dick." I turn and look at Smith walking out of the gym with his arm around the redhead's waist. "He screwed his way into that brownstone and I'll never forgive him for stealing it away from me."

Chapter 2

Smith

Brynn Bishop.

That name has been haunting me since I saw her at the gym yesterday. She may have thought I didn't notice her looking at me, but I did.

I type her name into every social media platform I can think of on my smartphone. The results on each of her profiles are the same. Everything is set to private. The only hint into her world is one visible picture of her. It's a tightly cropped image of her face in oversized sunglasses. There's no mention of her fiancé. I don't see a single picture of the elaborate wedding in the Hamptons that was planned for last summer. She didn't have a ring on her finger at the gym yesterday, but she could have slipped it back on after her workout.

Frustration pecks at me as I exit the browser and scroll through the emails that arrived in my inbox overnight. Not one of them is urgent enough to warrant my full attention. I close the email app and switch the phone's ringer back on. I silence it every night before I call it a day. I have to. My weekdays end earlier than anyone I know and as phone calls, text messages and emails roll in, I'm already clocked out, asleep in my bed in Brooklyn.

When you have to drag your ass out of bed before the crack of dawn five days a week, your bedtime rivals that of a four-year-old. I should know.

Earlier this year, I spent time at my sister's place in Kentucky.

My twin nephews are fed, bathed and dressed in their pajamas before most people in Manhattan have given dinner a thought. If nothing else, the ridiculous lights out before eight p.m. rule prepared me for my new job.

Being the co-host of Rise and Shine comes with a multitude of perks I'll never complain about. One is this chauffeured SUV. Hopping on the subway when I've just roused myself out of bed, is something I did in college, but no more.

I use these moments during the drive to the studio to go over the notes Resa, my executive producer, sends me thirty minutes before I wake up. It's a routine we established straight out of the gate when I took this job.

"Do you need anything, Mr. Booth?" My driver, a man with salt-and-pepper hair and a slight English accent, asks as he peers at me in the rear view mirror. "We have time to stop for a coffee. I know how much you hate what they serve at the studio."

He knows that because he heard me complaining over the phone to Resa two mornings ago.

My agent requested the essentials in my contract. That started with an eight figure a year salary and the non-negotiable role of associate producer. I want a say in the stories I'm bringing on air. He also secured a decent sized dressing room and office, one Friday off a month, my suits and shirts custom tailored from Berdine, the premier men's wear store in the city, and a driver who was supposed to keep the small talk to a minimum.

Good coffee wasn't mentioned, but unless Resa replaces the shit they've been serving me, I'll comment live on air about my love for the premium blend at Roasting Point, a family run chain of New York based cafés. I have little doubt that a plug to our daily audience of several million will benefit the owners of the business enough that a free cup of their coffee will never be more than an arm's reach away.

"I could use a decent cup." I reach forward to tap Arthur on the shoulder. "There's a twenty-four-hour Roasting Point a block over on Broadway. Pick up one for yourself too. Bill it to my expense account."

"You have excellent taste, sir." He replies with a curt nod. "Is there anything else you need?"

That list is a mile and a half long. It begins with a redo of the last twelve hours of my life and a miracle. Arthur isn't equipped to deliver either. "Just the coffee."

He pulls the car into a tight spot a half a block from the café. "I'll be but a minute."

"Take your time." I glance at the watch on my wrist. The same watch my younger brother gifted me on the day I graduated from college.

The car door slams shut just as my phone chimes. I look down at a text message from Caprice, the woman I spent a fun and forgettable afternoon with before I hopped on the subway eight hours ago to head home.

She wants more than I have to give her. Yesterday was the second time I went to her place. It was also the last.

A heart emoji at four a.m. does nothing for me. I delete her message suggesting we hook-up again tonight.

Stroking my chin, I scroll through the hundreds of names in my contact list before I land on Julian Bishop. We haven't seen each other in years. That changes today. I make a note in my calendar to call him once I'm off the air.

Catching up with an old friend will get me back on track. Hearing about what his beautiful younger sister is up to can't hurt either.

Chapter 3

Brynn

"I'm not sure pairing lavender walls with this pattern is the best way to highlight this room," I say with a smile.

I am sure that it's a horrible idea and if a picture of this Park Avenue penthouse bedroom sees the light of day, my career will be toast. It will be done when it's just begun. I'm finally starting to get recognition for my work. I won't let this purple catastrophe take me down.

"I had my heart set on that for the bedding, Brynn." Mrs. Pentlow, my client, whines. "I think the magenta in this fabric complements the color we chose for the walls."

I think the magenta in the fabric is burning my irises.

"You chose the color for the walls before you hired me," I point that out because there's no way in hell I would have even considered the hue as a wall color. I love the shade, but this bedroom is larger than most apartments. The tone isn't subtle enough for a room this size. It's overpowering. "I think if we want the room as a whole to be a statement, we need to use muted colors and patterns for the bed coverings and accessories. Let's make the wall color the star of the show."

She thinks that over with a furrow of her brow and a scratch to the side of her nose with a periwinkle manicured fingernail.

"I have some artwork that is to die for, Mrs. Pentlow." One of the pieces is not only striking, but it's large. It's big enough to cover most of the bare wall we're facing. "I want this room to be a sanctuary that you can retreat to at the end of the day."

"Is it expensive artwork, dear?"

Money is the measure of happiness for too many people in this city. I purchased two of the pieces from Bridget Grant, an emerging artist. She recently opened a small gallery in Tribeca. Charcoal portraits are her calling and the custom pieces she did for me of Mr. and Mrs. Pentlow will make the space that much more personal. I gave her two photographs of the Pentlows I found in their living room as a starting point and she worked her magic. The finished framed pieces are expensive, but not unreasonable.

I can't say the same for the Brighton Beck painting that will cover the wall we're looking at now. That was a fortune. It stands to reason since Beck, as he's called by his fans worldwide, commands more than six figures for every watercolor on canvas he creates.

"I think you'll be pleased to know that a few weeks from now, a Brighton Beck original will be the first thing you see when you wake up."

Her husband should be the first thing she sees, but judging from the fact that every stitch of his clothing is in the guest bedroom, I'd say Mrs. Pentlow is breaking the bank to create a room-to-die-for that will accommodate just one person.

Mr. Pentlow and the glass tumbler that holds his dentures will most likely continue to reside down the hall in a guest bedroom that hasn't seen the stroke of a paintbrush since sometime in the late eighties.

I mistakenly barged into that room during my second visit to the penthouse under the assumption no one was home. A toothless and pants-free Mr. Pentlow is a sight I'll never forget.

"As I told you, dear, money is not an object." She flashes me a grin. "I'm pleased that you see fit to incorporate a Beck into this room."

I make a mental note to call Mr. Beck's assistant this afternoon to ask how much purple is in the painting I commissioned. "I have several other surprises in store for you."

I don't at the moment, but since Mrs. Pentlow is leaving for Greece tomorrow, I have two months to complete this project before she returns from her fifth honeymoon.

"Let's do a grand unveiling when the Mister and I get back from our trip." She narrows her eyes at me. "You'll have it all done by then, won't you?"

With what she's paying me, and the promise of the rest of the apartment as an incentive to stay on time and budget, I'll have this bedroom done within the next two weeks. "I promise that you'll be stunned by what you see when you get home."

"Good." She coughs, clearing her throat. "Don't put your personal life on hold for this, Brynn. A woman needs time with her man, if you know what I mean."

Sadly, right now, I don't. I haven't been with anyone in a few months. My last relationship was short lived and as boring as watching paint dry. "There's no man in my life at the moment."

"No man?" Her voice raises an octave. "We live in Manhattan, Brynn. This is the city of a million possibilities."

"I'm focused on work right now." I shrug. I get that it sounds pathetic, but the only person I have to fall back on in this life is me. It's career before cock in my book. "I don't have time to go out and meet men."

"You don't have to plan an excursion to meet a man." She smooths the side seam on the skirt of my black dress. "They're everywhere. At the museums, Times Square, hell, you can even meet a man on the subway. Tell me the last place you saw an attractive man."

"At the gym," I blurt out without thinking.

That's what happens when I have Smith Booth on the brain.

"What did he look like?"

Like every dream I had when I was a teenager.

"He has black hair and brown eyes," I confess.

"I bet he has a body like my Morty did back in the day. I called him the Drill Sergeant." She leans in closer dropping her voice to a whisper. "It wasn't because of his time in the Army."

Silence fills the space. I'm stunned and she looks lost in thoughts about the man Mr. Pentlow used to be.

"That's a story for another day," she finally says. "Make a move the next time you see that fellow at the gym. You never know where it will go."

I know exactly where it will go. If I make a move on Smith Booth it will be a knee to his groin. He'll hit the floor and I'll walk away feeling completely satisfied.

Chapter 4

Smith

Julian Bishop, wearing an expensive tailored suit and sporting a five hundred dollar haircut, can't keep his eyes off a curvy dark haired woman who just walked into the restaurant. That, in itself, isn't a big deal. She's cute. She's also not the woman he's been involved with for the past few years.

"Do you know her?" I finally ask because someone has to break the trance he's in, and since we're the only two at this table, that job falls on my shoulders. I need to hit the hay in an hour. I don't have room in my schedule to wait around while Julian mentally undresses the petite woman wearing the red dress. I need to order dinner now if I have any hope in hell of making my self-imposed curfew.

"Maya Baker," he says her name without looking away from her. "We met last year."

Julian's not the fuck and tell type. I'm going to read between the lines and assume met is code for screwed senseless.

"Looks like Maya's on a date," I point out because I'm an asshole like that. Besides, the minute hand is inching closer to lights out for me. I need his undivided attention so I can ask about his sister.

"So it seems." He follows Maya and her date as they casually hold hands and walk across the restaurant. "What do you think he does for a living?"

I know exactly how he earns a paycheck. Julian's crush is having dinner with Everett Faulkner, the most widely sought after criminal defense attorney in the country. I interviewed him two weeks ago. My competition on the other networks called it a coup. I called it a favor. Everett owed me and I cashed that ticket in by asking for a sit-down, live on air, at eight a.m. last Monday. He was happy to oblige.

He gave me insight into the case he recently won. His defense of a senator's son accused of murder was brilliant.

"That's Everett Faulkner." I sip from the tumbler of whiskey I ordered. "I take it you know about the Carney case."

"That's Everett Faulkner?" He whips his head back to look at me, curiosity knitting his brow. "His work is impressive. No one thought he'd get an acquittal for Bert Carney."

Irritation brews within me. I didn't invite Julian to dinner to discuss this. I had one goal in mind when I suggested he meet me at Nova, my favorite restaurant in Manhattan.

I want to know what's happening in Brynn's world. I'm looking for insight into the life of the woman I saw yesterday. I need to nip this off topic discussion we're having in the bud now.

I should have gone with my gut instinct and asked the research department at the show to find her number. Hell, I know it's crossing a line, but it would have been a more efficient use of my time.

"I'll introduce you." I let out a sigh. I'm pulling from personal experience here. If roles were reversed and one of my past hook-ups walked in with a dude I didn't know, I'd bow out of the introductions. Shaking the hand of a man currently fucking a woman I once had my dick in, is not high on my to-do list.

Julian may see it differently, but I'm hoping the offer will put the issue of Maya Baker to rest.

"That's not necessary," he says right on cue as he turns back toward me. "I don't want to disturb them. The last I heard Maya was dating a doctor. I'm surprised that's over."

I can't resist the obvious question. I don't judge anyone else's life choices, but my curiosity is gnawing at the corner of my brain. I know it's not going to shut up, so I need to ditch the idea of getting to sleep at a decent hour.

"Did you hook up with her when the doctor was in the picture?"

"I've been with Isadora for three years, Smith."

That's the best answer-non-answer I've heard in weeks. I met Isadora once. From what I remember she's tougher than a two dollar steak. The woman is all business, all the time. It's paid off for her in spades, professionally.

"How is she?" I ask before I signal to the server that I want another drink. If Julian's about to wax poetic on the woman of his dreams, I need to settle in for the long haul.

Fuck sleep. I can survive on a couple of hours if need be.

"Fine." His gaze lands just over my shoulder.

What is this *fine* shit? The last time I asked about his beloved I was treated to a thirty minute sermon on the virtues of Isadora Patel.

"What's going on with you two? I thought you'd be married by now." Twisting my head to check on Maya Baker, I catch her giving Everett a chaste kiss on the cheek.

"Don't you need to get up early to be on the air, Smith?"

If I was a bigger dick than I am, I'd point out that fair maiden Maya is likely going to spread out in her birthday suit on a bed later tonight as Everett's dessert. I tone it down because Julian and I go way back. That reminds me why I invited him here in the first place.

"I have time," I say flatly. "How are your parents? I haven't seen them in years."

What can I say? I'm sensitive. I'm also smart enough to know that interrogating him about his younger sister right out of the gate will raise red flags. I'll ease into my questions about Brynn.

"Good. Busy." He looks down at his trillion dollar watch. Thousand dollar maybe, but still it makes mine look like a dollar store discounted special. "Yours?"

I have no fucking clue. Since my parents retired, they've been on a non-stop party-until-we-drop world tour. The last I heard they were in Australia, learning how to surf. "They're living the good life."

"They deserve it." He finally tears his eyes away from Maya again to look at me. "I'm proud of you, Smith. You took that college radio gig and turned it into a career."

I did. A few lucky breaks along the way didn't hurt. A year and a half as a midday news anchor in Buffalo turned into four years as the co-host of an entertainment show in Los Angeles. I've spent the last two years as the six o'clock anchor on a cable news network. My current job is the dream for me.

"I appreciate that, Julian." I pick up the glass of whiskey the server just brought me. "I don't have to say how impressed I am by what you've done with the hotels. I can't turn a corner without seeing a Bishop property."

"Expansion is my goal." He mirrors my movement with his glass and takes a drink. "The hotel chain has been in the family for years. I took it nationwide. The next step is to go international."

I see an opportunity so I take it. "I remember your mom being part of the business? Did your sister sign up too?"

"Jane's moved on to other endeavors." He smiles when he mentions his mom. "Brynn was on board right after she graduated. She quit last year to start her own interior design firm."

"Interior design?" Why the fuck didn't I find a trace of that online? I searched Brynn Bishop in two different browsers, three different times, after my scavenger hunt of her social media profiles turned up nothing. The only explanation is that she's using her married name now. Fuck if I can remember the name of the guy she was head over heels for.

"She has an eye for it, not to mention a master's degree." His gaze drifts back over my shoulder in Maya's direction. "The company is Brynn Janie Interiors."

"Brynn Janie," I repeat back. Janie's her middle name.

"She's determined to make it on her own. She thinks the Bishop name will give her a leg up. She's right but she's bull headed. She wants to prove she's got the talent to succeed."

It's impressive. Bishop is a name that commands respect in this city. To willingly toss it to the side is admirable.

"I could use some help in that area." It's not a lie. I've got a shit eye for design. I can't pair a shirt and pants together most of the time. The jeans and blue button up shirt I'm wearing right now are a testament to that. I stick to the basics when it comes to what I think looks good. Trying to decorate an entire home is a joke for me. "Maybe I'll give her a call."

"I'll text you her number." He picks up his phone from the table. "I can't say if she'll remember you. It's been years since you've seen her."

Wrong. I saw her yesterday and I haven't been able to stop thinking about her since.

I ignore the comment. Self-torture isn't my thing but I can't resist. I need to know she's happy. "How was her wedding? It was in the Hamptons last summer, right?"

He tosses back the rest of his scotch. "Brynn called it off the day before. It was the best decision she's ever made. I couldn't stand the prick she was engaged to."

Best decision indeed.

"What are we doing here?" He pulls his wallet from the inner pocket of his suit jacket before he tosses a hundred dollar bill on the table. "Let's go grab a beer at Easton Pub. We can order something to eat there."

I'm all for following him to the pub we used to hang at when we were in college.

He gives one last look in Maya and Everett's direction before he pushes back from the table. "Are you seeing anyone, Smith?"

"I'm not your type," I joke. "Maya Baker is."

He laughs, it's rough and low. "She's a talented real estate broker. We met in her friend's photography studio. We spoke briefly. End of story."

He's delusional if he thinks that's the end of their story. He wants her. He's convinced himself otherwise but Manhattan is a more intimate place than most think. Their paths are bound to cross again.

"The answer to your question is no, Julian. I'm not seeing anyone. Why?"

"I believe you asked my assistant out the last time you came to my office. I hoped that would go somewhere."

"It went to hell." I chuckle. "She was a fun one, but we weren't compatible long term."

"That might explain why she quit without a reason." He squints at me as he stands. "One day you'll find the right woman."

I might. I'm not convinced there's a perfect woman for every man. I am sure as shit that at some point tomorrow, I'll be talking to Brynn. With any luck, she's as single as I am.

Chapter 5

Brynn

"I love him, Ad." I hear my voice cracking. "I can't lose him. My heart can't take it."

"Brynn, listen to me." Adley York grabs my bare shoulders. I was in such a rush this morning that I threw on a strapless white dress and slipped my feet into a pair of worn out flip flops. I didn't even bother to brush my hair. "He's not going to die. We're going to start him on a cycle of antibiotics. I'll show you how to administer them. If you're not comfortable doing it, I'll come by your place before and after work to handle it."

"You'd do that for me?" I feel tears well in the corners of my eyes. Since I met Adley six months ago in the elevator of my apartment building, we've become good friends. We're almost the same age. We're both single and when either of us needs a shoulder to cry on, the other is there in an instant.

Adley lives two blocks from me. Fate put us together in the elevator that day. She was on her way down to the lobby from a disastrous dinner date with a guy she'd met at work. I was on my way out to have a drink with a man I didn't have anything in common with.

I called my date to cancel and Adley and I went for martinis. Our bond was formed that night.

"I'd do anything for you." She swipes her finger across my cheek to catch a tear. "Pike has an infection. You did the right thing bringing him in first thing this morning. He's not young, but he can fight this. He's strong. You know that."

I do know that. Pike, my sweet little brown and black Yorkie, was an adoptee. I don't know his exact age, but I know that his time is coming to an end. I'll fight with everything I have to keep him with me as long as I can. I won't let him suffer. If he's in pain, I'll let him go, but he's still as spry as he was eleven years ago when I first met him.

"Did Dr. Hunt get the test results back?" I look toward the brown haired veterinarian Adley works for. Two women are talking to him. It isn't surprising. The waiting room is always filled with women and their pets looking for a minute or two of the good-looking doctor's time.

He has a following on social media that has reached several million. I admit I'm one of them, but it's only because the last time I brought Pike in for his check-up, Dr. Donovan Hunt took a selfie holding my dog. Pike was a star for a day-and-a-half on Instagram before an overweight cat stole his thunder. Dr. Hunt flexed his bicep in that photo and there was a sudden rush of single women bringing their cats to the clinic to be evaluated.

It keeps Adley busy. Being an assistant to Dr. Hunt is a stepping stone to her dream of becoming a vet herself.

"Most of the results are in." She looks down at the tablet in her hand. "It's a stomach bug. It's not uncommon, but you need to make sure he's drinking plenty of water and I'll give you a couple of cans of food. Feed him that until his stomach calms down."

"Will do." I nod as I cradle Pike in my arms. "Is there anything else I should be doing?"

"You should answer your phone." She gestures toward the large brown leather purse slung over my shoulder before she pushes a strand of her blond hair behind her ear. "It's ringing again."

"It's nothing important."

She tucks the tablet under her arm and reaches to take Pike from me. He instantly nuzzles into her chest. "Someone thinks it's important enough to call twice in the past five minutes. See who it is so you can be sure it's nothing."

I sigh heavily as I fish in my bag for my phone. "It's probably Mrs. Pentlow checking in to see if I've found a man yet."

"Isn't that the woman you're doing design work for?" Adley smiles, her blue eyes brightening. "Are you taking relationship advice from her now?"

"She was offering advice. I wasn't asking for it." I glance down at my phone and the incoming, unfamiliar number. "This might be a new client. I should take it."

"Take it." She looks over at the reception desk. "I'll get that prescription ready and pack up the food. Once you're done your call, find me and you can take this little guy home."

I nod, stepping to a quiet corner of the waiting room. I clear my throat, calm myself and answer the way I always do. "Brynn Janie Interiors."

"Brynn Bishop. It's been years. "His voice is pitched low, rough, and as sexy as I remember. My face flushes and my insides knot in ways I've never felt before.

"Who is this?" I ask, even though I know exactly who it is. Every cell in my body can sense the energy that's coming from him. It's palpable. Smith Booth's voice hasn't changed. Its effect on me hasn't either.

He huffs out a surprised laugh. "You know exactly who it is."

Charming egotistical asshole is still a part of his repertoire. Bitchy brat is still a part of mine when need be.

"Matthew? I've been thinking about you," I purr.

It's not a lie. I have been thinking about Matthew. He's a friend and a recent client. I redesigned his home office in rich dark tones and imported woods. He paid me my going rate and let me drag a professional photographer to his apartment so I could add the before and after images to my online portfolio. The sexual tension between us ranks below zero, but Smith doesn't need to know that.

"No. It's not Mathew," he replies flatly.

I take a deep breath. I'm tempted to end the call, but knocking Smith's ego down a notch or two is worth the anxiety I'm feeling talking to him. I pull the name of my dentist from out of the ether. The only thing about me that Dr. Tony Adami is interested in is my slight overbite.

"Tony, it's you, isn't it? Do you want to meet for drinks? I'm available now."

"It's not even noon, Brynn." His words come out as a warning.

I jump in before he can say anything else. "We can skip the drinks and go straight to your place."

"Jesus." The sexy rasp in his tone sends shivers down my spine. "How the fuck is this conversation happening? I'm not Tony."

I smile. Toying with Smith is fun, but I have a full day of work and taking care of Pike ahead of me. "My bad. Whoever you are, it's been a slice, but I need to run."

"You know who I am." The sound of a blaring horn punctuates the words. New York traffic is a familiar third voice in many conversations in this city. "Drop the act, Petal."

Petal.

He's the only person on the planet who has ever called me that. It started more than a decade ago when he caught me plucking the petals off a bouquet of daisies my middle school boyfriend had brought me. It wasn't a game of he loves me; he loves me not. I was in shock that day, knowing that Rhett Marin, the boy who had hand delivered the flowers, had kissed my best friend the day before. I knew he didn't love me. I doubt he even liked me very much. The flowers were a token gesture meant to patch my broken heart.

He'd used me to make my friend jealous and when she ignored him after that kiss, he turned back to me as his consolation prize.

Smith walked into our sun filled apartment on a bright Tuesday afternoon in early summer looking for Julian. Instead, he found me sitting next to our ornate dining room table with dozens of daisy petals at my feet.

He called me Petal and Rhett became a distant memory, replaced with an instant infatuation with my brother's best friend.

"Smith Booth," I whisper his full name. "What do you want?"

"You're not even going to ask how I am?"

I don't care how he is. I care what he did. A phone conversation isn't going to erase his past deeds. He can't undo the damage.

"I'm busy, Smith. I can't talk right now."

"I saw you at the gym." The thud of a car door slamming in the background draws my eyes to the street outside the vet clinic. He's likely miles from here. Manhattan may be an island, but there's always a way to avoid someone you don't want to see. Some people don't believe it's possible, but I know firsthand, that it is. I've been doing it with Smith since he got back to New York City. I was successful until yesterday when he walked into my gym.

"I didn't notice you," I lie.

"Bullshit." He sighs. "You saw me. Why didn't you say hello?"

Because I hate you. Except I don't.

"I didn't see the point." I motion to Adley that I need another minute. She kisses the top of Pike's head.

"I want to see you." He exhales sharply. "I'm on my way to a meeting, but let's set a time now. Tell me when we can talk."

"There's nothing for us to talk about." I rub my fingertips across my jaw as I grind my teeth together.

"You're wrong." His voice lowers. "I thought we were friends. I know I hung out with Julian when we were younger, but we were friends too, Petal."

Friends? Friends don't stab each other in the back and twist the knife until it pierces the heart.

"You're Julian's friend. You were never my friend."

"That's not how I see it." His deep voice is husky. "I have to get into this meeting. Give some thought to sitting down with me. It could change your life."

He already changed my life in immeasurable ways.

I don't bother with the expected goodbye. Instead, I end the call, toss my phone back into my purse and try to reason away the pounding of my heart and the hunger for the man I've despised for the last three years.

Chapter 6

Smith

Matthew? Tony? What the actual fuck happened when I called Brynn?

I called her out on her bullshit, but now, a day later, I'm second guessing whether she knew it was me on the phone or not. If not, I have my work cut out for me.

I don't doubt that I can compete with any man in her life. I have the secret weapon of friendship on my side, although she threw that back in my face before she hung up on me.

She's pissed. She has every reason to be. I shut her down when she was seventeen and drunk on cheap vodka. She tried to kiss me at Julian's birthday party, I dodged her lips and I've regretted it ever since.

She was too young. I was too loyal to her brother and once that ship sailed and I left for Buffalo, I pushed the memory of the moment to the back of my mind.

"A yearly membership to the gym would be a more economical option for you, Mr. Booth." The attractive blond behind the counter points out as she hands me back my credit card. "I can sign you up right now with a special discounted rate."

"Is Brynn Bishop a regular?"

The question catches Heidi off guard. I assume her name is Heidi. That's what the small name tag pinned to the front of her tight yellow T-shirt reads.

"I can't disclose any information about our members, sir." She licks her lips as she looks at my mouth.

"She's my best friend's younger sister." I have no fucking problem using this woman's attraction to me to get more information on Brynn. If I make her believe my interest in Brynn is platonic, I stand a good chance of getting her to forget the rules and answer my questions. Having a face that women see first thing in the morning has its advantages. Fame comes with its own set of fucked up benefits and this is one of them. "I saw her here the other day but I didn't get a chance to say hello."

"Julian Bishop is your best friend?" Skepticism knits her brow. "If that's true, when is his birthday?"

How the fuck does this woman know when his birthday is? "September eighth."

She eyes me up. "That might be a lucky guess. What else can you tell me about him?"

"He'll be on Rise and Shine next Thursday during the eight o'clock hour." I lean an elbow on the counter. "He's going to announce that he's breaking ground early next year for the first Bishop Hotel in Paris."

The interview isn't a done deal yet, but we're close to making it happen. Julian reached out via email this morning to give me the heads-up. I asked for a sit-down and he's rearranging his schedule to accommodate. He'll make it happen. It's a great piece for me and an excellent marketing opportunity for him.

"You actually know him, don't you?" Her eyes widen. "What I wouldn't give to work for that man. Can you put in a good word for me?"

Since I know absolutely nothing about Heidi, other than her stalker like fascination with Julian, I'm leaning toward not sending her his way. "You want to work for Bishop Hotels?"

"They're rated one of the five best companies to work for in the country." She lets out a quiet laugh as if I'm an idiot for not knowing that. "I still can't understand why his sister didn't jump at the chance to work for him."

Heidi knows too much about the Bishops to just be the receptionist at this gym. "How well do you know Brynn?"

"Well enough to know that she's here almost every Monday, Wednesday and Friday at four o'clock." She taps the plastic strapped watch on her wrist. "Lucky for you, she's mid workout at this very minute."

***

"Brynn."

Her entire body stiffens when she hears her name coming from my mouth. She's standing next to the same treadmill she was on when I first saw her here days ago. Her back is to me, but I can guarantee that the look on her face is priceless.

There are at least ten seconds of silence before she responds. She doesn't turn to look at me but her words are loud and clear. "Leave me alone, Smith."

I rake her body. Today she's dressed in a pink tank top and black yoga shorts. She's everything I remember, right down to the small tattoo above her left elbow. One simple word encased in a heart. It's a word that means everything to her; family.

"Turn around." I reach forward to touch her but stop myself because if I feel her skin, I won't be able to control what happens next.

That's a lie. I never take what isn't offered willingly to me. I know she still wants me though. I see it in her labored breaths.

Her shoulders slump forward. "I'm about to do thirty minutes on this treadmill. I don't have time for you today."

"I'm not asking for eternity here." I step closer to her. "I'm asking for two minutes to clear the air."

She spins around and looks at me like I'm the clown from her tenth birthday party. Confusion, anger and curiosity are all layered in her expression. Her eyes land on the black tank top I'm wearing before they skim over my bare arms. They're impressive. I know it. Petal knows it too. The sudden blush washing over her cheeks tells me she likes what she sees.

"Two minutes?" Her index and middle finger jut into the air. "Two? You're fucking joking. Tell me you're fucking joking."

I've never heard that word come from her lips. My dick hardens instantly and I move the towel in my hand to cover up. A stiff cock isn't going to help me in this situation.

That's a statement I never expected would cross my mind.

"I'm serious." I widen my stance and raise a brow like I'm all kinds of right and she's wrong. She is. My only crime is that I didn't kiss her years ago. It's not like I ruined her life.

"You're an asshole."

There's a fire in her that I don't remember. This isn't the Petal I rejected. This woman is different, bolder. Apparently, when I dodged her kiss, I left a mark on her heart. It makes me want her even more.

I lose the towel and step closer, not caring that my cock has pitched a massive tent in my gym shorts.

Her eyes drop. "What are you doing?"

I rest a finger on her chin, tilting her face up to me. "I'm going to right my wrong. I was an idiot back then. I should have done this all those years ago."

I lean down, eager to kiss her mouth. Her eyes widen as her lips part. "Smith, are you going to kiss…"

"What the hell, Smith?" A sharp toned female voice interrupts the moment from behind me. I feel a hand on my shoulder, nails digging into my skin. "You fucked me two days ago. Did I mean absolutely nothing to you?"

Obviously, since I told her as much before I screwed her, both times. I wanted a hook-up, she seemed into it. Apparently, I read that wrong.

Brynn backs away, her gaze glued to the hand on my shoulder.

"Answer me, Smith." The woman behind me pushes against my back.

I turn and face her, reaching to grab both her wrists as she moves to punch my chest. "Caprice, stop. Just stop."

"Stop?" She literally screams the word in my face. "You never answered the text I sent you the other night. I've been waiting to hear from you. I can't believe you were going to kiss her when you and I have a thing going on."

The only thing we have going on is we're currently the center of attention in this gym. All eyes and several phones are on us. In my business, that's publicity I don't want. I have a public image to uphold, along with a paragraph in my contract that states I need to keep my shit together, so I don't embarrass the show or the network.

"Let's discuss this calmly, Caprice." I lower my voice. "Give me a few minutes to clean up and we'll talk at the pub across the street."

"I'd rather talk at my place," she mewls.

In other words, she'd rather fuck at her place.

"The pub, Caprice," I insist with a dimpled smile. "I need a drink. You look like you could use one too."

"We'll talk about going to my place, right?" Her eyes drop to the front of my gym shorts and thank fuck that my cock's interest is solely in Brynn. It's still impressive under the fabric, but at least it's not bordering on obscene anymore.

"Go change and meet me at the pub in fifteen minutes." I drop her wrists.

"I'm on my way." She pivots on her heel and takes off in a slow jog across the gym, her red hair bouncing off her shoulders.

"Look, Brynn." I take a deep breath as I turn. "I'm sorry…"

My voice trails. She's gone. I scan the entire gym but there's not one trace of Brynn Bishop anywhere.

Fuck.

Chapter 7

Brynn

The lash of a sandpaper tongue on my cheek awakens me. I turn to the side and reach out to pull him close. He jumps back, playfully pawing at my hand. I open one eye to see Pike's little brown eyes staring at me.

"You're feeling better, aren't you?" My voice cracks with emotion. "You're the strongest boy I know."

I'm rewarded with a bark and a whimper.

"You need your breakfast and your medicine," I say it as much to myself as to him. It's seven a.m., but I've only been asleep for an hour. Work and thinking about Smith Booth stole a good night's sleep from me.

I went straight to the Pentlows' empty apartment after I watched the exchange between Smith and his current lover in the gym yesterday. I walked away once I heard her remind him that they're involved.

He almost kissed me.

I almost let him.

I don't know what came over me, but I wanted the kiss. I wanted it as much as I did when I was a teenager. Smith barely knew I existed then. Yesterday was different. He sought me out at the gym. Heidi, the receptionist and a classmate from high school, told me as much as I was racing to get out of there.

He came there looking for me. He said he wanted to right the wrong but a kiss isn't going to change anything between us.

You can't kiss away a broken dream. It isn't that simple.

My phone buzzes just as I round the corner to the kitchen. I glance down at the screen and a notification that I have a new email. It's my work account. Since I only have one client at the moment, and she's somewhere in the Mediterranean with her Drill Sergeant, I put Pike down on the floor and open my email app.

I skim the message quickly, my gaze bouncing back to the sender several times. I rub my eyes before I read it again.

Is this real?

"Are we awake, Pike? I feel like I'm dreaming." I smile down at him. He's jumping on my legs, a subtle reminder that I promised him a meal.

I open one of the cans of dog food Adley gave me and empty a portion into Pike's ceramic bowl. I pinch a small amount of the soft food between my thumb and forefinger and push one of the pills Dr. Hunt prescribed into the middle of the bite of food. I bend down and feed it to Pike who eagerly swallows it before he eats every morsel in the bowl.

"I'll take you for a walk once I look at this email again." I pick up my phone and read each word of the email slowly. Then I do it again.

"You're up early." Sydney walks into the kitchen dressed only in a pink bra and panties. "Do you need to get to work? I can take Pikey for his walk."

I love that she adores my dog as much as I do. I couldn't ask for a better roommate. She's still in college, and now that she's on summer break, she's devoting her time to working as a barista.

"I was just about to take him." I look down at the short yellow robe I'm wearing. "I need to get dressed first, obviously."

She laughs as she reaches into the fridge to pull out a small bowl of fruit salad. "I'll save half of this for you. You should eat breakfast more often, Brynn. It's the most important meal of the day according to my dad."

Her dad is a cardiologist and his health advice always finds a way to seep into Sydney's good intentioned lectures. She's a clean eater who tries to stay away from anything with sugar or alcohol. I'm always joking with her that her virtue cancels out my sins. At least when it comes to food and cocktails, it does.

She does indulge from time-to-time and I was lucky enough to be the one to buy her a vodka and cranberry juice on her twenty-first birthday. We had a blast and our friendship has only strengthened since then.

"Read this email and tell me what you think it means." I push my phone toward her. She pops a piece of cantaloupe into her mouth as her gaze scans the screen.

"Brynn?" Her amber eyes light up. "Are you joking? You know exactly what this means."

"I think I know what it means. I need you to tell me it's real."

She places my phone down on the quartz countertop and tugs me into a tight embrace. "It's as real as it gets. Brynn Janie Interiors just landed the job of the century. You're about to become the most well-known interior designer in all of New York."

***

I walk past the security guard with my temporary visitor badge on full display. It's strung around my neck from a bright red lanyard that clashes with the light blue dress I'm wearing. I don't care how I look right now because the badge is my ticket inside The Beryl, the most widely anticipated residential development in Tribeca in years.

After I received that email this morning from an assistant to the developer of the project, I took Pike for a walk around Central Park. I wanted to reply immediately, but I've learned that appearing overeager is never a good thing in business.

Anna, the assistant to Cooper Lannen, the developer, made it clear that Mr. Lannen had exactly thirty minutes to talk to me this afternoon. She was sparse with the details in the email she sent, but I read enough between the lines to know that my incessant emails and phone calls to him have paid off.

The Lannen Group NYC put the word out four months ago that they were considering hiring an up and coming interior designer to take on the task of creating a show suite for The Beryl. It's been called a risky move within the industry, but Mr. Lannen and his children have never played by the rules.

I haven't either so when I decided to throw my design hat into the ring with the thousands of others who want this job, I took a different approach. I didn't just create computer generated renderings of the two bedroom unit.

I transformed my bedroom and attached bathroom into my vision of what I pictured as the master suite of a space elegant enough to be considered as part of The Beryl. I made a video with the help of a friend who is enrolled in film school. As I walked through my bedroom and master bath, I spoke extensively about where I would source the materials for The Beryl from. I mentioned the psychology of creating a space for someone who wants to live in the heart of Tribeca. Then I moved on to spatial concepts and the necessity of creating customized units, so potential buyers will feel an immediate connection to the building the moment they walk through the doorway of the show suite. My goal was to create an experience that would strike a chord with Mr. Lannen himself. I've studied his past projects. I spent time understanding his vision of residential properties and I incorporated that into my pitch.

It was an expensive and risky gamble. I knew that even if I didn't land the job, I increased the value of my own apartment in the process. My dad might be impressed if he knew what I was up to.

I haven't said a word to him or Julian. They both know Cooper Lannen and that could have been my ticket to the top of the short list for this project. I never wanted that. I knew I could land this job on my own. I'm good at what I do. I've been obsessed with interior design since I was a little girl always asking my parents to take me to the furniture store that was two subway stops from our apartment.

The exposure from this project could send my business into the stratosphere.

I finally replied to Anna's email just before lunch telling her that I was still interested. She sent me a message back almost immediately inviting me to meet with Mr. Lannen at two o'clock.

As I trail one of Mr. Lannen's assistants toward a bank of elevators my gaze catches on a group of workers huddled around a marble column. They're putting the finishing touches on the remodel of the building and hopefully I'll be showcasing all of their hard work by creating an environment that will convince people to open their wallets and pack their belongings so they can call The Beryl home.

Landing this job will make me a household name in this city. My face will be recognizable and my business will explode. This meeting that I'm going to have with Mr. Lannen will be the most important of my life.

I take a deep breath, smile at his assistant and follow him into the barren show suite once we exit the lift. Mr. Lannen is standing in front of a wall of windows. His back is to me, his phone next to his ear. This is it. As soon as he's done, he's going to change the entire trajectory of my life.

Chapter 8

Brynn

"You know that I'm a Bishop?" I furrow my brow. "How do you know that?"

Cooper Lannen chuckles. "Julian told me all about your design business when he toured one of our other projects a year ago. I commended him on the seamless opening of the Bishop Hotel on Fifth Avenue. I mentioned how much I loved the interior design and he told me that you'd had a hand in that."

I had more of a pinky finger than an entire hand in that.

Julian hired one of the design firms who he's worked with for years to handle the interiors of the hotel rooms and the lobby. The building itself has so much rich architectural history that it made the job of the design team simple. They played off the hotel's innate charm to create rooms that are elegant and sophisticated.

My one and only role on that job was to oversee the area rugs in the lobby.

I may not have put my stamp on the space, but it was a notable addition to my portfolio.

"So, as I was saying." He pockets his phone. He took another short call after telling me I had the job. I was grateful when his phone rang. It gave me the minute I needed to swallow back the rush of emotion I felt bearing down on me. By the time he ended his call, I was back in control, or at least I appeared to be. My heart is still racing. I can practically hear its beat in my ears. "I talked it over with my kids and we all agreed that your pitch stood out from the rest and I need to say I respect the fact that you don't depend on your surname professionally. Your father has a lot to be proud of when it comes to you."

He might be. I wouldn't know. We don't talk business.

"My children are taking over the business next fall." He shakes his head and looks past me at the blank canvas that I'll soon transform into the show suite that a broker will use as an integral part of the marketing campaign to sell out the building. "It's not easy for me to hand the reins of my life's work over to those three."

I don't know any of them. I've read about Mr. Lannen's children, but that was only because I wanted to understand the full scope of the business. Each of his two daughters heads a specific division within the company and his son is in charge of international acquisitions. Even though Sonya Lannen runs the residential developments, her dad took the lead on this building. I can see why. Cooper's proud of The Beryl. That's evident in the care he's taking with its launch.

"I can't imagine how that must feel, Mr. Lannen," I admit. "I don't have any children."

"They're more trouble than they're worth." He hides a smile behind his fingers as he touches his gray beard. "I love my kids but not enough to give them control of this building. This is my last hurrah and you're just the girl to help send me off into retirement in style."

I know I am. I'm going to kick ass so hard on this project that when his children are in the market for an interior designer in the future, Brynn Janie Interiors, will be the only name on their list.

***

"I think I have to find a new gym to work out at," I mutter as Adley and I sit down on a bench in Central Park.

It's her lunch hour and since I'm not meeting the contractor I hired to help me with the closet in Mrs. Pentlow's bedroom for another two hours, I thought we could spend the next sixty minutes gossiping our way through a quick meal of a sandwich and lemonade.

I'm fast tracking the Pentlow project now that I've landed the job at The Beryl. I've been over the moon since yesterday. I even skipped my session at the gym to go out for a celebratory Bellini after my meeting with Cooper.

I eyed up the pub across the street from the gym and headed to their outdoor patio instead of to the treadmill I usually devote my late afternoons to. My ass might not thank me, but the rest of me enjoyed my mini-celebration even if I did spot Smith going into the gym just as I took the first sip of my drink.

"Why? I thought you liked that gym?" She takes a generous bite of her turkey and avocado on grain bread and chews.

"Do you remember when I told you about Smith Booth?" I look down at the untouched pastrami on rye in my lap. I skipped breakfast again today, even though Sydney had scrambled some eggs before she left for work. She gave half to me and after I'd picked at it for a full fifteen minutes, I pushed the plate away. I've had zero appetite since Smith reappeared in my life.

"The guy from Rise and Shine?" She finally asks after she swallows. "He's so hot, Brynn. Like holy hell hot."

"He's not that hot," I say quickly.

"Lie to yourself if you want, but he's got that certain something going for him." She shakes her head and blows out a puff of air. "If you weren't secretly crazy about him, I'd ask you to introduce me."

"I'm not secretly crazy about him." I roll my eyes. Everything I've told Adley about Smith is related to why I can't stand him. I needed to get all the anger and pent up frustration I was feeling off my chest after I spotted him on one of the massive screens in Times Square a few months ago. He was conducting an interview on the cable newscast he used to anchor. I blurted out who he was and why I hated him. Adley stood silently next to me repeatedly nodding as I sobbed my way through my past with Smith Booth.

She washes down another bite of her sandwich with a sip of lemonade. "You know what they say about the thin line between love and hate."

"Who are they and what do they say?"

"They are people who have fallen in love with their sworn enemy." She throws her arm around my shoulder. "It's true though, Brynn, love and hate come from the same place in your heart. You had a crush on this guy and then he crushed your dreams. Maybe you need to face him, give him the shit he deserves and see what happens."

"He acts like he doesn't remember what he did to me." I pick up half of my sandwich before I place it back down on the paper napkin in my lap. "It pisses me off. I wanted that brownstone. He knew it and he still went ahead and bought it."

"Brynn." She softens her voice. "I know that house meant a lot to you, but your grandma would totally get what happened. She wouldn't want you to carry this hurt around with you. I never met her, but I'd bet a hundred dollars that she'd tell you it's time to let it go."

I wish more than anything I could hear my grandma say those words to me.

"You bought a kick ass apartment. You're making a name for yourself in this town. She'd be super proud of you."

"I hope that she'd be," I mutter.

She sighs heavily. "If you forgive Smith, you'll feel better about all of this. I guarantee it. You'll be able to look at him and not want to strangle him."

Forgiving Smith feels impossible, even if a part of me is wildly attracted to him. Since Adley is in the mood to hand out advice, I make a confession. "The other day at the gym, Smith was about to kiss me."

"What did you say?" Her hand squeezes my shoulder so tightly I wince. I won't be surprised if her fingernails tear a hole in the white blouse I'm wearing. "You didn't mention that. Why the hell did you not tell me that?"

I glance at her. Her face is lit up in a full smile. "It's not a big deal. I was trying to work out. He walked in and started to lean down to kiss me and then…"

"And then what?" She pats my jean covered knee with her fingers. "Tell me what happened next."

"His lover walked in and gave him hell," I reply with a roll of my eyes. "End of story."

"That's not the end of the story, Brynn." She moves to grab her sandwich. "I think your story with Smith is just beginning."

She's wrong. Whatever happened at the gym between Smith and I was a one-time thing. I doubt he'll ever try and kiss me again. Even if he does, I'll resist. I think I will. Won't I?

Chapter 9

Smith

Brooklyn is where I belong. This is where I put down roots when I came back to New York City. The energy here rivals Manhattan, but the pace is slower, the street art vibrant and the people here aren't all in a rush to run over each other to grab the brass ring.

Sure, competition is still a thing in the neighborhood I live in, but the mom and pop shops that line the streets are each unique in their own way. I should know. I've stopped to talk to hundreds of people who live and work here. A few of them will become the focus of an upcoming feature I'm doing on the show about the lives of Brooklynites.

"Smith?" Mrs. Denson, the woman who owns the bakery next door to my building, taps me on the shoulder as I walk into her shop. "I baked a half loaf of that wheat bread you love. You want it now, son?"

I smile as I lean down to kiss her cheek. "Pack that up and a couple of those sugar donuts Mavis loves."

"Mavis doesn't deserve you, you know that?" She drawls in her thick Brooklyn accent as she rounds the counter to get my order. "I told her yesterday that you're never going to propose. Do you know what she said to me?"

I laugh as I pull out a few bills from my wallet. "What?"

She carefully places two freshly made sugar donuts in a small brown paper bag. "She asked if I remembered Tommy from around the way."

"Tommy?" I perk a brow.

"Back in the day, Mavis and Tommy had a thing." She pats the top of my hand. "Years before you were born, dear."

"What happened to Tommy?"

She leans one elbow on the glass display case that's holding dozens of pastries baked in the cramped kitchen in the back. "Who knows? I told Mavis he'd never marry her but he popped the question and a month later, poof, he was gone."

"Gone?" I swallow hard. "He died?"

She throws her head back in laughter, the gray hair framing her face moving with the motion. "Nah, but I should have killed him myself for running off with Loretta Jansen. Last I heard he was living somewhere in Ohio."

I know I should take off, but Leona Denson's stories are too good to pass up.

"He broke Mavis's heart." She mimes cracking her own heart apart in front of her chest. "I'll never forgive him for that."

I rub my chest. "I won't break her heart."

"I know, son." She pushes the clear bag containing the half loaf of bread at me. "You love my sister almost as much as I do."

"You're right." I turn to leave. "Thanks for the bread and donuts. Keep the change."

She looks down at the bills on the counter. "You're too good to me, Smith. I'll see you the day after tomorrow."

She will. Just like clockwork, I bring Mavis a donut every two days. My elderly neighbor looks forward to it almost as much as I do.

***

"So we're going to pretend like we don't know each other?" I swipe a white hand towel over my bare chest. "How long do you think you can ignore me, Brynn?"

She doesn't look my way. She completely disregards every word I just said and keeps up her pace on that damned treadmill she seems attached to. I had my eyes glued to it for the past hour. When she waltzed into the gym, dressed in a pair of bright red yoga shorts and a matching sports bra, I almost pounced on her. I didn't. I kept lifting, my eyes glued to her.

I watched as she stretched before starting on the treadmill. She worked her way up to a full run within minutes and hasn't slowed since.

Her high ponytail bounces as she keeps her gaze on a guy with a shaved head deadlifting little more than a hundred pounds. I could do that with one arm tied behind my back. I have, actually. I did just that on Rise and Shine on my second day on air. I know what hikes the ratings and me, shirtless, is one approach that works to drive the show's numbers up.

"Fine," I say on a huff. "Listen while I talk."

She keeps up the fast pace. Her flawless legs moving gracefully as she nears the five-mile mark.

"I don't have anything going on with Caprice." I decide to start there because I want her to know that

I'm not a guy who kisses one woman when he's regularly fucking another. "We hooked up but I didn't make her any promises. I set her straight the other day when we left the gym. Nothing's going to happen between the two of us again."

She straightens her shoulders, her back arching slightly.

I doubt like hell she even cares about Caprice. It's not like Brynn has given me a signal that she wants anything to do with me.

I shake my head. I need to say it. If I say it now, she'll understand where I'm coming from. We can put the embarrassment she felt when she was a teenager behind us and start over.

I want that fresh start. I need it. I spent more than an hour yesterday telling Mavis about Brynn. She said that as much as she wishes she was forty years younger, she wants me to be happy and Brynn sounds like the woman to make it happen. I'm not convinced of that. I'm attracted to her but goddammit this woman hates the fuck out of me right now.

"I'm sorry, Brynn," I say it loud enough that I know she can hear it over the incessant hum of the machine. "I fucked up. I never meant to hurt you. Forgive me. Please."

She slows. She finally slows to a fast walk before she takes the tempo down even more. It's then that she looks at me.

Her expression is impassive. Her eyes scan my face looking for something. It might be more details, but I'm not going to drag up the past to humiliate her. We both know what happened that night.

I was in the kitchen of the apartment Julian had bought right before his birthday. We'd graduated from college a few months before, but our partying days weren't behind us. Julian reached out to a few guys he still hung out with from school and told them to bring whoever the hell they wanted. The alcohol was on his dime so the party grew and Brynn, who showed up unexpectedly with a friend from high school, ducked into the kitchen to steal another splash of vodka for her orange juice.

I caught her. I took the bottle away from her, she slurred out a few sentences about me being a big bully before her words and the look on her face shifted to something else.

She reached up, grabbed my shoulders, leaned in and closed her eyes.

I admit I considered kissing her.

She was seventeen.

I was twenty-two.

Taya Morgan was in the next room waiting for me. She was my girlfriend at the time.

I called a car service and when I stood on the curb outside the building watching Brynn and her friend drive away, I felt like shit. She was one month, two days and ten minutes away from being eighteen. She was also the younger sister of my best friend.

I was a lifetime away from understanding what I let slip through my fingers that night.

She steps off the treadmill and stands in front of me. The angles of her face may have changed since that night and her brow has softened, but she's just as beautiful now as she was then.

"You're actually sorry for what you did?" Her gaze drifts over my chest before it lands on my face. "Do you know how much it hurt me, Smith?"

"I do," I admit on a sigh. "I never meant to cause you pain, Petal. I need you to know that."

She bites her bottom lip as she studies my face. "You stole my dream, Smith. You just took it and stomped all over it."

I don't know what to say. I've thought about that night from time-to-time, but over the years it became a distant memory. When I found out from Julian that Brynn was planning her wedding, I admit I considered reaching out to her to see if any of the sparks that were there that night still existed. I dropped the thought from my mind as soon as I realized that her happiness isn't something I want to fuck around with.

If kissing me was her dream, I'm about to make it a reality.

"I tried to right my wrong the other day. I'm going to do it now." I reach down and grab her hip, pulling her closer.

"How are you going to right your wrong?" She whispers as she looks up at me with those intense blue eyes. "Some things can't be fixed."

I run my tongue over my top lip. "Let me try and fix this."

I lean down, anticipation coursing through my body. My dick stiffens. My senses shift to high alert. I smell the soft scent of her perfume, catch a quick glimpse of her pebbled nipples under her sports bra and I swear she moans when I cup the back of her neck with my palm.

"Do you really think a kiss will fix this, Smith?"

It's a start. We're both adults now, so a nice long fuck will chase the bad memories away, but I'm a gentleman.

Kiss first. Fuck second.

"You've wanted to kiss me for eight years," I whisper against the shell of her ear. "I've wanted it too."

She pushes hard against my chest with both hands, separating us instantly. "I've wanted to kiss you for eight years? Says who?"

"You?" I shrug. She plays the part of the wounded heroine like an Oscar winner. "You wanted me when you were a teenager. You want me now. Nothing's changed. "

"What?" She mutters under her breath, her hands leaping up to cover her face. "What the hell?"

"Brynn?" I reach out to touch her shoulders, but she backs up. "I'm trying to fix this. You're obviously pissed at me so I'm going to kiss you and then we can finally leave the past where it belongs."

She throws her head back as a hearty laugh escapes her. "Seriously? You might be a great kisser, Smith, but it's not a magic eraser. You can't undo the past with a kiss."

What the fuck? Does this woman want me to get on my knees? Do I have to beg for her forgiveness because I stayed loyal to my girlfriend and passed on the chance to make out with her in a cramped kitchen uptown?

"You're making a bigger deal out of this than it is," I say gently, trying to defuse the situation. My sister had a broken heart when she was fourteen. I get that it can stay with a person for years, but this is ridiculous. Brynn was engaged to another man. She fell in love with someone else. She needs to move on and forgive me. "You need to get over it. Let it go already."

"Shut up," she says hoarsely, her voice breaking. "How can you say that? It was a big deal. It will always be a big deal."

I don't try to stop her as she turns and walks away. There's no way in hell this is about what happened in Julian's kitchen years ago. I broke her heart in two. I wish to fuck I had a clue how I did it.

Chapter 10

Brynn

It's been an hour since I saw Smith at the gym. I'm on the sidewalk across the street from the brownstone that I once imagined would be my home. I haven't been here in years. I couldn't bring myself to walk down this street, so I avoided it, tearing my way through Manhattan as if East Sixty-Seventh Street never existed.

Years ago, I'd make a point of walking this block at least a few times a week. I'd daydream about the dinners I'd cook there and the holiday gatherings that would take place in the grand sitting room.

In every single dream, there would be a familiar face beside me. She'd be there when I got home from work each day. She'd help me pick out which accessories complemented the furniture pieces I'd chosen for my clients.

Those dreams died the day my broker told me that the seller had accepted another offer. I knew it was Smith who had sealed the deal. I'd insisted on speaking to the seller myself, but Otto, my broker told me that the contracts had already been signed.

Smith Booth bought the townhouse I planned on bringing my grandmother home to. It was the same place her mother had wanted to live but her time inside was restricted to ten hours a day when she took care of the household needs of the wealthy family that lived there.

My grandmother spent her summers in that house when she was a kid. She sat on the floor playing with wooden puzzles and reading books as my great-grandmother peeled potatoes, washed windows and ironed the clothes of the people she worked for.

A loud cough behind me startles me enough that I turn. It's a friendly face; older and distinguished.

"Are you lost, Miss?" The man I'm looking at touches the lapel of his white suit jacket. "We don't get a lot of folks standing on this block for so long."

I have no idea how long I've been here. It's been long enough to notice the front door of the brownstone is now painted a dark brown. It once was blue; the same shade as my eyes, my mom's eyes and my grandmother's too.

"I once knew someone who spent time in that house." I wave my hand toward the brownstone I thought I'd be living in. "I was just remembering the stories she told me."

"I take it they were good? If they weren't, I doubt you'd be standing here staring at the front door."

I manage a faint laugh. "They were good. I wish I could hear them again."

I'll never be able to. My grandma is gone, just like my chance to live in that house and build my own memories.

"I tell my wife all the time that every crevice of this city has its own story to tell. If the walls of that home could talk, you'd hear those familiar stories and more."

I nod as my gaze catches on the tall man walking up the street. He's carrying a shopping bag filled with groceries in one hand. The other is cradling his phone next to his ear.

He's not dressed at all like he was at the gym. Smith is wearing jeans, a dark T-shirt and sunglasses. His gait is easy and relaxed.

"That man right there could tell you a story or two about that place." The white-suited man points in Smith's direction. "He worked his fingers to the bone restoring that townhouse. He's on the news. He's a big shot. Booth Smith is his name."

Close enough.

"He didn't work his fingers to the bone," I correct him because my great-grandmother was the one who worked her fingers to the bone in there. She worked every single day, including Christmas Day and Easter Sunday to provide a stable income for her two daughters after her husband died.

Smith made a few calls, ordered a latte and let the professionals bring that four-story building back to life while he soaked up the sun in Los Angeles. "That man hasn't done a day of manual labor in his life."

"I hate to disagree." The man next to me taps his chin. "I watched him work alongside the contractors almost every weekend for more than a year. He can wield a hammer with the best of them."

I cringe. My mind jumps to a place it shouldn't be. I can't keep staring at Smith whenever I'm near him. He may be incredibly good-looking and built like a sex god, but so are a lot of the men in this city. I need to stop looking in his direction.

"Would you like me to introduce you to him?" he asks excitedly as Smith nears the brownstone. "It would be my pleasure."

No. It would be Smith's pleasure because he'd think I'm hanging out in front of his home because I'm desperate for him to kiss me. In his mind, I've wandered aimlessly through life for the last eight years bereft because I was never gifted with the taste of his lips.

Jesus, the man's ego is bigger than Manhattan.

"Thank you, but that's not necessary." I watch Smith tug a set of keys from the front pocket of his jeans before he unlocks the brown door and steps inside. "I have nothing to say to Smith Booth."

***

"Why don't you two just hate-fuck already?" Adley scoops Pike into her lap. "I've never done it, but I hear it's mind blowing with the right person. Or maybe it's the wrong person since in order to hate-fuck, you have to technically hate the person you fuck."

"What?" I try to make sense of what she just said. "You're not saying that if I have sex with Smith that all my problems will be solved?"

"I've yet to meet a man who can fuck every problem away." She pets Pike's chest before she kisses the top of his head. "All I'm saying is that you're mad at him, he wants to kiss you and you're both obviously hot for each other. Just do it already, Brynn."

I glance down at the screen of my phone and the text message Smith sent me an hour ago.

We need to talk, Petal. Meet me at Easton Pub at seven. You know the address. You got caught inside the place with that shitty fake ID you had when you were seventeen. In case you forgot, I was the one who saved your ass that night. You owe me and I'm cashing in now. Seven sharp.

I don't owe him a thing. He came to Easton Pub that night because he was the one who answered Julian's phone when I called. Julian was on a date and had forgotten his phone at Smith's apartment. Smith arrived just as the owner of the pub was about to call the police to report me since I refused to leave. My rebellious stage was not cute.

Smith came and resolved the situation. He did it as a favor to Julian.

"Go and talk to him." Adley points at my phone. "Clear the air. Scream at him if you have to. If anyone else had bought that brownstone, you would have forgiven them. You're hanging on to this because you feel something for him. I see it. He sure as hell must see it when you two are in the same room."

"That's ridiculous," I scoff. "If I feel anything for Smith it's hatred."

"You couldn't hate a person if your life depended on it." She puts Pike in my lap. "I'm going to make us a salad. You'll eat and I'll keep Pike company while you go talk this out with Smith. Do it, Brynn."

Chapter 11

Smith

Brynn walks into Easton Pub thirty minutes late. She looks like something out of a dream. Her body is covered in a short white shirtdress cinched at the waist with a simple silver belt; her feet are in silver heeled sandals. Her gorgeous long legs are on display. They're toned, tanned and all I want is to feel them wrapped around me as I fuck my name from deep in her throat.

She glances around like she doesn't notice me at the bar. I planted myself here when I arrived an hour, and two glasses of whiskey, ago. I saved the seat next to me despite the fact that two different women offered to keep it warm. I turned them down easily even though I'd normally invite them both back to my place.

Experience has taught me that the quick way to breakfast in bed for three is to flirt the fuck out of both prospects and let the cards fall where they may. I've been known to take all that's offered. It's never been more than I can handle, until now.

Brynn Bishop is the only woman I want tonight and judging by the look on her face, I'm the last man she wants anything to do with. Her gaze catches briefly on the suited guy on stage singing the shit out of "*Oops…I Did It Again.*"

Wisps of her pinned up hair fall around her face when she finally makes eye contact.

I wave her over, willing my dick to behave. The bulge in the front of my jeans is big enough to warrant attention from the woman who just walked by me. I'm not interested in her. It's Brynn that my body craves.

Her eyes skim over my face and the black T-shirt I'm wearing. I dress down when I'm out in the evening. Women still give me a second glance, but when I've ditched the tailored suits, they don't make the immediate connection that I'm the dude they drool over when they're eating their breakfast cereal every morning.

My hair isn't styled in place as per Rise and Shine standards tonight. I showered, ran my hands through it and left my apartment looking like I was ready for a fuck.

"What do you want, Smith?" Brynn's sapphire blue eyes cut through me as she approaches. This woman's eyes always got me. They may be the same color as her brother's but their depth is endless. The contrast to her jet black hair is striking. She's seriously the most beautiful person I've ever seen.

"Sit, Brynn. Have a drink." I pat the seat of the wooden stool next to me.

"I don't want a drink."

"Said you, never," I deadpan. "Are you still drinking vodka and orange juice? If you are let me introduce you to a new friend. His name is Jack Daniels."

She eyes the vacant stool. "I'll stand. Tell me why you ordered me down here."

"I'm sorry I didn't kiss you when you were seventeen." I muster as much sincerity as I can find in the bottom of the second empty glass of whiskey. I know that death stare she keeps throwing my way isn't just about the kiss, but that needs to be cleared off the table before we go any further down the list of reasons why she can't stand me.

I tap my glass on the wood bar to get the bartender's attention. I want a refill but I need to slow down. At this rate, I'm going to ditch my sense of what's right and wrong and end up on stage for amateur karaoke night. A viral video of me trying to catch the high notes of, "*My Heart Will Go On*," wouldn't necessarily be a bad thing.

She levels me with a stare. "Why are you stuck on that non-kiss, Smith? I forgot all about it until you brought it up at the gym."

I call bullshit with a red flag. "You didn't forget about it."

She tosses me an exasperated smile with a sigh of impatience. "I forgot about it when I went home that night and kissed Leon Sibley."

"You kissed Leon Sibley?" My hands clench into fists. Motherfucking Leon Sibley was at the party at Julian's. He showed up on the coattails of his older brother. Leon was a sophomore at NYU at the time, with an end goal of one day becoming a doctor of some discipline I didn't give a shit about back then. He was background noise, bitching about the ill effects of all the alcohol I was consuming and the bag of weed that found its way into one of the guestrooms.

He was a nuisance, an annoyance I wanted gone. Apparently, Brynn viewed him differently.

"He followed me home." She meets my eyes. "He had the doorman call me after I went in. I ran right down to see him."

She better not give me a play-by-play of what happened. I don't want to hear it. Sibley saw an opening and moved in. That's all I need to know.

"It was the most romantic first kiss in the world…" she hesitates, looking over at the guy giving his all as he belts out yet another Britney hit. "He wrote a song for me. He sang it before we kissed."

Who does shit like that? Wait. Her first kiss? She was seventeen at the time.

"I didn't know Sibley had it in him," I say, my voice not giving anything away. "He was your first kiss, Petal? What about the jerk that broke your heart and caused the death of the dozen daisies I caught you ripping to shreds?"

"I never kissed Rhett." She squints at me and then gazes at the drink the bartender just placed in front of me. "First kisses are supposed to be special. Rhett wasn't special."

I was. Goddamn my life to hell. She wanted me to kiss her. She was almost eighteen-years-old when she made her move on me and I brushed her off, sent her home and into the waiting arms of that crooning idiot Sibley.

"I should have kissed you," I murmur as I watch her reach forward to pick up the glass of whiskey before she takes a mouthful.

Her shoulders lift, her neck bows back and her eyes close as the liquid burns her tender throat. Her tongue swipes her bottom lip before she finally looks at me. "You should have but you didn't. It's all for the best. I got one of the best kisses I've ever had and you… I remember Julian saying something about you getting dumped the next day."

I did. Taya dumped my ass the next night with a weak excuse about needing space. I accepted the job in Buffalo; ran through my training for my first on-air job and screwed my way through as many of the single women in the city as I could.

"The kiss was that memorable?" I wrap my hand around the glass and swallow what's left.

She kissed another guy after I turned her down. I could have been that sweet memory that will forever own a corner of her mind. I should have been her first kiss, her first fuck, her first goddamn everything.

"His lips tasted like blueberries." She arches a perfectly shaped brow as if to challenge me.

I don't know how to respond to that. *Blueberries?* Who the hell wants to kiss a blueberry? If I would have kissed her that night she would have tasted raw need with a pure lust chaser. I wanted her. I convinced myself it was wrong, but I wanted her. I would have waited until she blew out the final candle on her eighteenth birthday cake to have a taste of those lips. I should have.

"It's all for the best. It's in the past, Smith. Let it go."

I can't. I know there's more simmering inside of her. She's full of rage whenever she's near me and even though it's hot-as-fuck, it's also annoying. I want it gone. I want her to see me for who I am now, not whoever the hell I was when I pissed her off.

"I'm done talking about that night," she says indignantly. "It's not like either of our lives would be any different if we would have kissed back then."

I can't stop myself. I'm not done talking about it because she just dropped a bombshell in my lap and I don't have a drop of whiskey left to chase down the bitterness of the bad choice I made eight years ago. "Your life would be different now if we would have kissed back then."

Her eyes widen. "You're wrong. Nothing would be different now."

"You don't know that." I exhale roughly, irritation gnawing at my gut. I'm not pissed at her. I'm the one who turned her down. My life is the one that would have been different if I would have pushed my reservations aside and taken a taste.

She rests her hand on my shoulder as she steps closer to where I'm still seated on the stool. I shift, parting my knees to give her access. She takes it, moving until she's standing between my legs. "A kiss is just a kiss, Smith."

"You know that's not true, Petal."

"I'll prove it," she whispers before she cups my face in her hands, tilts her head and sweeps her soft lips over mine.

Chapter 12

Brynn

He takes control of the kiss almost immediately. His hand grabs my hip, the other cradles the back of my neck. He angles me the way he wants, the taste of his lips controlling me. I'm intoxicated by the scent of his skin and the mild jolt of whiskey that peppers his tongue as it glides against mine. He moans into my mouth and my knees weaken. My body heats and I melt at the same time.

Goose pimples pop up on my arms, my legs, and every single spot that I want to feel his touch.

I step even closer to him and he growls out my name. He wants more and dammit, I do too.

I can't.

This is Smith Booth.

I almost whimper as I pull back and break us apart.

His lips breeze over my cheek, leaving a soft trail of kisses that land on my ear. "That was worth the wait."

No, it wasn't. Shit. Yes, it was. That's why I tossed all common sense aside and went for it.

I've never been kissed like that. My ex-fiancé couldn't make my panties wet with just a kiss.

I resist the desire to kiss Smith again. I did it to prove a point to him and all I accomplished was to get myself so worked up that I'll need to come the second I close my bedroom door tonight.

I take a step back because I don't trust myself. "It was just a kiss, Smith."

"Are you trying to convince yourself of that?" he asks. His eyes are dark as he looks at the outline of my hard nipples through my dress. "You felt what I felt, Petal. Don't deny it."

So I felt aroused? Big deal. I haven't been with a man in months. It's not surprising that a kiss would ignite something in me.

"I kissed you to show you that a kiss is just a kiss." I reach to pick up my clutch. I'd tossed it on the bar when I made my move on him. "Now that we've settled that, we can finally stop talking about what didn't happen when I was seventeen. Agreed?"

"No," he says matter-of-factly. "I won't agree to that unless you agree to have dinner with me."

Like that will ever happen.

I kissed him to make him shut up about that night at Julian's when I was still a teenager. None of this changes anything between us. He stole the brownstone from me and I can't forgive him for that.

"I will never have dinner with you," I say coolly, my heart finally finding a beat pattern that doesn't mimic a tap-dancing troupe on a tin roof.

"Why not?" he challenges with a smirk.

Because you'll only hurt me more. You know every weakness I have and you're at the top of the list.

"You know why," I hiss out through clenched teeth, my nostrils flaring. "You keep acting like you didn't fuck me over, Smith. Maybe in your world you get by with just ignoring your wrongs until everyone else does too, but that's not how it is with me."

He draws in a deep breath and then releases it slowly, his eyes never leaving my face. "I need you to explain to me what I've done. Tell me, Brynn, because I have no fucking idea why you hate me."

I chew on my bottom lip contemplating how to respond. I can't tell if he's genuine or not. If he is, that means that all the anger I've held inside me for years has been in vain. Maybe he doesn't even remember that he stole my dream right from under me.

"If the looks you've been giving me could kill, I would have been dead days ago." He shoves a hand through his messy black hair. "I can't stand that you're in pain because of something I did. At first, I thought it was what happened at Julian's place years ago, but I get that it's more than that. Tell me. Petal, just tell me how I fucked up."

I hate that I kissed him just now. I hate that I want to again, but mostly I hate that I have to confess something to him that he should already know.

"You really don't know?" I ask softly, leaning in so he can hear me over the woman singing the final verse of, "*Like a Virgin*," at the top of her lungs.

He looks directly into my eyes. "I swear I don't know."

Knowing that hurts almost as much as the moment my broker called to tell me the home I wanted so desperately had slipped through my fingers.

I texted one of my dad's associates almost immediately once I got the news the brownstone was sold. I wanted the name of the buyer and he wanted me to put in a good word for him with my dad. He reached out to a couple of brokers he knew and within the hour I had the confirmation I didn't really need.

The buyer was Smith Booth.

I didn't discuss any of it with my dad because my opinion matters little to him. I got what I wanted out of the agreement and it changed what I felt for Smith from that moment on.

I turn to the stage as soon as I hear the beginning chord of "*Sweet Caroline.*"

It was my grandma's name.

Caroline. Sweet Caroline.

I can't bear hearing her name right now.

"I'm leaving." I turn back to Smith. I've thought over and over about the moment I'd eventually confront him about what happened. There was never once a scenario in my mind where would he say that he had no idea why I'm upset. I assumed that he was living under an umbrella of guilt for taking away something so precious that was within my grasp. I've had it wrong all along. I don't know what to make of that or what I'm feeling after that kiss.

"Do you want me to come with you, Brynn?"

The question catches me off guard. I should want to walk away from him right now. I need to take some time to think through what's happened between us tonight. Instead of telling him I want to be alone, I look into his eyes. "If you want to."

He stands, his hand circling my waist. "I want to more than anything. Lead the way."

***

My first thought was to take Smith home. Not with me and not so we could round third base even though that's the only thing that consumed my thoughts my senior year of high school.

I wanted to take him to his home; the brownstone on East Sixty-Seventh Street where I should be living with Pike. As soon as we hit the sidewalk outside Easton Pub and I felt the lazy heat that fills summer evenings in New York, I changed my mind.

I craved the calm that comes from the city. Some people find it chaotic and loud. To me, it's the center of peace. When I need to think there's no better place for me than outdoors, even in this jaded, unpredictable city.

Going to Smith's place would mean I'd see all the rooms that my grandma wanted so desperately to see again. I want that, but right now my mind is reeling. I'm still trying to process the kiss, not to mention the fact that Smith seems oblivious to the reality that he stole something from not only me but my grandma too. She wanted to live in that brownstone and spend the rest of her life in the house that she always imagined she'd call home.

She first told me about it when we were hurrying down a quaint street on the Upper East Side on a rainy afternoon when I was in college. She stopped mid-step to stare at the façade of a home and I could tell by the look of enhancement on her face, that the building owned a piece of her heart.

I pushed for more details and over the weeks and months that followed, she told me tales of her mom and the work she did there. I smiled when she explained how she and her sister would spend summer days in the kitchen of the brownstone when my great-grandmother couldn't find a neighbor or friend to take care of them.

I laughed when my grandma told me that she'd written her name on the inside of the pantry door. It was a tangible sign that she'd grown up in that home in a very limited, restricted way.

The picturesque red-bricked townhouse brought a light to her face; a face that had aged beautifully and gracefully even though her body and mind had become worn with the passing years.

"Where are we going, Petal?" Smith's voice breaks through the mountain of memories.

I look up at him. I want to ask him about Sigrid Hull, the woman he bought the brownstone from. She was a model at the time and he was the host of a nationally syndicated entertainment show. Their paths crossed at a charity fashion show here in New York. He was based in Los Angeles back then, but for some inexplicable reason, he bought her place.

He knew I wanted it. I'd reached out to him twice asking him to arrange a meeting between Sigrid and me. I left messages for him both times explaining the sentimental value that property held for my grandma. I wanted to appeal to Sigrid's heart after I'd put in my offer. It was full ask, all cash, with no contingencies and a thirty-day close.

I thought I had it within my grasp, but then Smith swooped in and signed on the dotted line, for less money, terms that didn't match mine and a list of contingencies a mile long. Two days later he escorted Sigrid to the Met Gala.

My grandma died three months later still holding onto the hope that she'd live in that house one day. She left me everything, including Pike, and the guilt that I couldn't fulfill her last dream.

"We're going to the top of the world," I say, finally. I don't need to add anything to it. There's no explanation necessary. Smith knows.

His mouth curls up in a soft smile. "I'll get us an Uber."

Chapter 13

Smith

The top of the world.
To most of the people in Manhattan it means the observation deck of the Empire State Building or the city-wide views at the top of Rockefeller Center. That's not what it means to Brynn and me.

"I can't believe you still have the key." I turn my head back toward the street. The financial district quiets only marginally after the closing bell of the day. Pedestrians still crowd the sidewalks and traffic streams by at a steady pace. I've kept my head low since we exited the car that brought us here. I don't want to be recognized now. Even though the sun has set, women still seek eye contact when I pass them. I admit I do the same if I'm looking for a brief connection in the seas of faces in this city.

"The key is our ticket to the roof." She jerks her thumb in the direction of the lobby. "I'll try and talk our way into the elevator, unless…"

She perks one of those dark brows in a silent question. I respond with a wiggle of both of my own. "This is going to be a walk in the park."

She laughs. This time it's genuine and fuck me, if it doesn't make her face light up. "The guards here aren't going to fall victim to your charm, Smith."

"I'll bet you I can get us into the elevator within three minutes flat."

Her gaze darts beyond the wall of glass and the manned security station near the bank of elevators. It's an office tower by day and at one time, the roof was home to one of the most exclusive bars in the city. "It's a bet. What do I get if I win?"

My cock has its own answer to that question. My mind and mouth go with a tamer response. "I'll buy you dinner tomorrow night."

"Is this one of those bets where the wager is the same on both sides?" Her lips twist wryly. "Are you going to tell me that if you win, you'll buy me dinner tomorrow night?"

It doesn't take a goddamn genius to realize I want to have dinner with this woman. I want to fuck her more than I want a meal, but I'm not about to mess up this moment by adding unrestricted access to my dick to the pot. That's a caveat that I'll offer her the moment she eats the last bite of her dessert tomorrow.

I still want her to clue me in on what I did to her. She left that conversation back at the pub and being the selfish asshole that I am, I haven't brought it up again. I stayed silent during the car ride here because I don't want to tarnish this adventure with a replay of whatever the hell it was that I did to hurt her.

I'll get to the bottom of it at some point. I need to, but right now I'm going to savor this for what it is; a chance for me to spend a few minutes with her where she doesn't look like she wishes I'd fall off the face of the earth.

"I can't fool you, Petal," I say on an exhale. "We have a lot to catch up on. I want to buy you dinner."

"I want something else."

So do I. I want you in my lap while I suck on your nipples and slide your wet pussy along my shaft until you're begging me to fuck you raw.

"What do you want?" I ask, my voice hoarse, sweat blooming on my skin from the mental image of her naked and ready for me.

She takes in a deep breath, pausing to look at the guard. There's no doubt in her mind that he's no match for me. She watched me talk the owner of Easton Pub out of calling the police when she refused to leave the bar after being busted with a fake ID. I convinced the man to let her walk out with a warning, even though he swore up and down that he was going to make an example out of her.

"If I win, you have to cook dinner for me tomorrow night at your place."

Brynn inside my apartment is a win for me. "You've got yourself a deal. Are you going to cook dinner for me tomorrow if I win?"

"The answer to that is no," she drawls through a small grin. "If you win I'll bring take-out from that burger place in Times Square you used to like."

How the fuck does she remember that I practically lived on those greasy burgers when I was a teenager?

"You'll bring me a cheeseburger, fries and a vanilla shake?" I ask pushing my luck. The elephant in the room is still squarely on my shoulders. Brynn wants to hate me, but her resolve is weakening. The offer for my favorite meal from a decade ago is proof positive of that. "You'll bring it to my place?"

"Deal." She holds out her delicate hand.

I shake it. Regardless of how this plays out with the security guard, Petal is going to be in my apartment tomorrow night. That's a win-win any way I look at it.

***

The key to the door that leads to the rooftop space is on a long silver chain that she tugs out of a zippered compartment in her clutch. It's not the only thing in there. I hear the distinctive sound of metal rubbing against metal as she draws the chain from her purse.

"So he didn't know who you were?" She asks me for the second time since she waltzed up behind me in the lobby and pulled some random dude's name out of a hat that she handed to the guard with a breezy smile and a wink. He waved us toward the elevator immediately even though I'd spent at least five minutes trying to convince him that I was the guy he sees every morning when he drags his ass out of bed to get his two kids ready for summer day camp.

"Rub it in again, Brynn." I stand right behind her as she places the key in the lock. "What name did you drop to get us in the building?"

"Crew Benton." She looks back and up at my face. "My friend Adley knows him. When I brought her up here a couple of months ago, she told me that he co-owns the building with his brother."

"You didn't think it might be worthwhile to mention that before I tried to charm the guard?"

She pivots, so she's facing me now, a smile playing on her lips. "And miss that show you put on in the lobby? Not a chance, Smith."

I clear my throat, my hands clenching into fists at my sides to deter the overwhelming urge I feel to reach out and pull her to me so I can kiss her again. "You won the bet fair and square so I'll be your personal chef tomorrow night."

"I'll text you a list of my food preferences."

I can't tell if she's joking or not. "I only cook one thing, Petal. It's spaghetti Bolognese or nothing."

"That's on my list of things I eat." She dangles the chain in her fingers. "Are you ready to see what the old Vernalt Social Club looks like now?"

"I'm as ready as I'll ever be." I take a step closer to her as she turns back around and slides the key in the lock.

I worked on this rooftop deck when I was in college. When the owner was around, I was busy bussing tables. The rest of the time, I was behind the bar opening beer bottles, washing glasses and downing a finger of the good bourbon whenever I got the chance.

I brought Brynn up here late one night when the world felt too heavy for her. I'd found her on the curb outside her parents' apartment, her face in her hands, her shoulders swaying with the force of her sobs.

I didn't ask her what was tearing her up inside. Instead, I waved down a cab, got her into the back seat and used the key my boss gave me to sneak her up here for her first sip of beer.

She told me that night that she felt as though she was at the top of the world looking down at a city full of hope. It was months later, after the bar shut down and I was on the cusp of graduating college that I found out what had happened. She'd been passed over for a summer internship at the company she desperately wanted to work for.

It was Bishop and Associates, her father's real estate firm. Fulton Bishop never saw the promise in his daughter that was always there. It still pisses me the hell off.

I left the key in an envelope addressed to her, on the kitchen counter in her parents' apartment the day before I graduated. I had no idea if it still opened the lock to our private rooftop retreat but it didn't matter. It was a token symbol of how the world was hers for the taking.

She didn't need her dad to succeed. I'm glad she sees that now.

"Follow me," she whispers with a crook of her index finger as she pushes open the door. "I think you're going to like what you see."

I already do. I'm staring at the most beautiful woman in the world and I'm seeing flashes of forgiveness in her eyes.

Chapter 14

Brynn

I turned immediately after I walked through the doorway so I could see Smith's reaction. I know that he hasn't been up here in years. Hardly anyone has. All the furniture and most of the lighting from the bar were removed eons ago. All that's left is a simple white string of lights strung over a fake tree of some sort that the bar owner's left behind. I added two mismatched chairs that I found on the sidewalk next to a mountain of trash bags last year. Neither of them is in good shape, but they beat sitting on the concrete staring up at the stars.

"What the hell?" he whispers under his breath. "Is this the same place?"

No one would ever know that at one time New Yorkers came up here to unwind. Relationships began and ended on this rooftop over a glass of wine. People met, left together and fucked in the hotel a block over before ending their nights with an awkward goodbye and the understanding that they'd never see each other again.

The same thing happens at every bar on this island.

"It feels even more like it's the top of the world now." I stare out at the expansive views of the city. "I come up here sometimes to think."

He nods silently like he understands exactly what I'm talking about. I know that he does. He's the one who brought me here to begin with. He poured me a quarter of a glass of beer and as he finished off the bottle, he gazed at the Brooklyn Bridge that night.

I let him believe it was my first taste of beer. It wasn't. I'd snuck a bottle that belonged to my dad from the fridge when I was barely fourteen. I took a sip before I washed the rest of the expensive imported beer down the kitchen drain as our housekeepers giggled.

Smith didn't need to know that. When he poured me that beer, he thought he was giving me my first taste of something forbidden. I did want a taste of something off-limits that night; his lips.

"The city hasn't changed that much since I brought you here the first time." He sucks in a deep breath, his chest straining against the T-shirt he's wearing. "You've changed, but the city always stays the same."

He's wrong. The city has changed just as much as I have. It's not only the sky high towers that developers are building to draw the millions that foreign investors are looking to sink into the city. It's much more than that.

People don't stop to talk to their neighbors the way they used to. Familiar faces you could always count on to be there have disappeared and the dream to make a mark on this tarnished, imperfect paradise is getting farther and farther out of reach.

"I grew up, Smith," I point out studying his profile as he gazes toward Brooklyn the way he did the first time we stood up here together. "I'm not the girl you once knew."

He swallows hard, his throat working on the motion. It's sexy for some reason only my body knows. It's reacting. I don't want it to, but I can't help myself. I haven't stopped thinking about what happened back at Easton's Pub.

How can a kiss shared with someone you hate feel so good?

"You don't have to tell me that," he says quietly. "When I saw you at the gym I couldn't believe my eyes."

I couldn't either. When I spotted him I was struck by a wave of something so intense that I could only push it into the cluster of hate that I've been carrying in my heart for years. It didn't fit there though. It was so much stronger than that. Desire and need, reckless want.

"I called your brother after I saw you. I wanted Julian to tell me that you were happy."

Julian wouldn't know happiness if it slapped him across the face. He's treading water in a relationship with a woman he thinks is perfect for him. She is, on paper. She doesn't challenge him or excite him. I see it whenever I'm in the same room with him and Isadora.

"What did he say?"

He turns and stares at me. "He told me that you dumped that tool you were engaged to. I assume that made you happy."

It did and it didn't. I broke up with Joel, my fiancé, the day before I was set to walk down the aisle. I couldn't commit to a lifetime of uninspired love and mediocre sex. I know now that I hooked up with him to try and drown out the pain I was feeling over my grandma's death. I was using him as a bridge to the other side of my grief.

When I called to tell him that I wanted to see him so we could talk things over, he already knew. I think he was relieved to hear me say that I didn't love him enough to marry him. He's engaged now to a woman he adores. I saw it for myself when I ran into them last month uptown.

"He wasn't right for me." Talking about Joel is always hard, even though I know ending our relationship was necessary. My parents saw it differently, shaming me for the expensive dress, venue and gourmet dinner for two hundred guests they'd already paid for.

I didn't let it go to waste.

I told the caterers to take the food to a charity that houses the families of ill children. They held a celebratory dinner that night, complete with the wedding cake that I was supposed to cut with my new husband.

I donated the dress, shipped my engagement ring back to Joel and told my brother to take Isadora to Paris, on what would have been my honeymoon. Julian focused some of his time during the trip on scouting locations for the Bishop Hotel that will open in France next year.

I paid my parents back every cent they'd invested into my non-wedding. I didn't want the constant reminders that I'd let them down so I evened the score and they dropped the topic.

"You're not seeing anyone now, are you?" His brows draw together.

How the hell is that his business? I'm still mad at him. I haven't forgiven him because his kiss made me forget my own name.

I have every intention of confronting him about the brownstone. I never toured the property when it was for sale. The only images viewable online were two of the red-bricked exterior. I thought about asking my agent to call the listing broker to arrange a private showing but I didn't see the point. To me it would have only been wasting precious time. I wanted it so I made the offer as quickly as I could.

Smith is my chance to get inside it now. I do want to see the rooms my grandma talked about. It seems fitting to call him out on the house he took from me, inside its walls. It may be bittersweet but I know I'll finally feel a sense of vindication. If I have to play nice tonight to make that happen, I can do it. I know I'll be stronger tomorrow when the kiss and the conversation we had at Easton Pub have both lost their edge.

I clear my throat to tell him that my dating status isn't his concern when his phone rings.

He tugs it from the front pocket of his jeans. "I usually mute this fucking thing before I go to bed at eight."

"You go to bed at eight?" I glance down at the silver watch on my wrist. "It's past your beddy-bye time. I should tell your mom you broke curfew."

He laughs at the reference to the words he used to say to me when I'd skip my midnight curfew to hang out with my friends. Julian would always be the one who'd track me down and order me home before my parents realized I wasn't in my bedroom.

All too often, Smith would still be at our house when I finally walked through the door.

"Dammit," he mutters under his breath. "I need to take this."

I nod before turning to the view of Brooklyn. I can't make out anything he says. It shouldn't matter to me if he's talking to another woman but it does. It niggles at me in a way I don't want it to. I've gone from outright hating him a few hours ago to tolerating him.

In an alternate universe we may have had a chance for something more but nothing can ever happen between the two of us. I let my grandma down because of him. She was one of the few people in my life who believed in me and I didn't pull through when she needed me to.

"Brynn." His hand lightly brushes my shoulder. "I need to go down to the studio. They're prepping Senator Carney for an interview tonight. I'm the guy he wants to sit across from him."

I turn and look up at him. "His son killed a woman in cold blood."

"The fucker did." He nods slowly. "The senator bought his son's freedom and I'm going to do everything in my power to get him to admit to that."

Smith's known for his hard edge. He pushes the people he interviews. If I was going to admire one thing about him, that might be it. The way he looks in a black T-shirt with the wind gently blowing his air might be another.

Get a grip, Brynn. Jesus.

"I'll see you at your place tomorrow night." I take a step back, so he doesn't make the assumption that my lips are looking for any goodbye action.

"I'll text you my address." His gaze drops to his phone at the sound of a chime. "Shit. My driver's downstairs waiting. I need to go before the Senator changes his mind."

"Go." I wave my hand as if I'm showing him the direction of the door. "I know where you live."

"You do?" His lips hint at a smile. "How? Have you been following me?"

Biggest ego in Manhattan.

"Don't flatter yourself," I say tightly, not wanting to feed it anymore. The fact that he even has to ask how I know his address irks the hell out of me. Obviously, my pleas to put in a good word with his former fuck buddy, Sigrid, so I could buy the brownstone were so inconsequential to him that he's completely forgotten them. I've been stewing over this for years and it feels like he's left it all behind him. "I saw you going into your building with grocery bags when I was in the neighborhood for work one day."

The work part is a tiny lie, although I did give my business card to Smith's white-suited neighbor. I have a feeling his townhouse may be a blank canvas, so it didn't hurt to offer up my services in case he ever needs a splash of color.

"You should have said hi."

"I'll come by before your curfew." I look at my watch, ignoring his comment. "Say around six?"

His phone chimes again. He mutters a chorus of curse words before he turns toward the door calling back to me. "I have a feeling tomorrow night is going to be one for the record books."

"Oh, it will," I whisper as I watch him disappear behind the door. "It's going to be a night neither of us will ever forget. Until tomorrow, jerk."

Chapter 15

Brynn

"You kissed Smith?" Adley's eyes widen. "You're telling me that you made the first move?"

I shake my head. "It wasn't like that, Ad. I kissed him to prove a point."

She grins. "What point? That you like him? That you want to get naked and sweaty with him?"

I can't admit that to her. I haven't fully admitted it to myself yet. That kiss kept me awake all night long. I replayed it in my mind like a lovesick school girl, which is still a part of who I am whenever Smith is within eye shot.

I want to hate him, but my resolve is fading. The kiss has a lot to do with that. The way he treated me afterward did too. He didn't push me in any way even though I could tell that he was thinking about the chip I'm carrying around on my shoulder.

"I tried to kiss him when I was seventeen and kind of drunk," I admit softly. We're in one of the exam rooms at the vet clinic and the walls are paper thin. I brought Pike in for a check-up on the advice of Dr. Hunt. I was grateful to see Adley's smiling face when I walked into the office.

"We all try and kiss someone when we're seventeen and kind of drunk. If we're lucky, they kiss us back. I take it Smith wasn't into you back then?"

I shrug as I pet Pike's head. "He says he regrets not kissing me eight years ago."

"What was last night's kiss like?"

I brush my fingers over my lips. "I can still feel it in a way. I know that sounds unbelievable, but I can feel his lips on mine. I've never been kissed like that before. It doesn't matter though. It's not like we can ever be together. Too much has happened between us."

"Brynn." Her fingertips tap on my shoulders. "I need to say something, but first I want you to know that I love you."

I pick Pike back up from the exam table and cradle him next to my chest. "Is it about Pike? Did Dr. Hunt tell me to come down here because something's wrong? I know you were still waiting for more tests to come back. Just tell me, Ad. Just say it."

"He's good." She pets that soft spot on his neck. "This is about you and Smith."

"What about us?"

"Dr. Hunt made the entire staff take a course on grief about a year ago. It was tough, but we needed it. We deal with death every day here."

I nod. "I couldn't do what you do. I'd be in tears every single day, all day long."

"I cry sometimes. It's impossible not to when you see people in that raw moment of loss."

I feel tears welling in my eyes as I think about how I'll deal with Pike's death when the time comes. It won't be easy. I don't think I can brace for it, but I'll have Adley to guide me through the grief.

"One of the things I took away from that course is that heartache set its own timetable. One person can grieve for a month, while another takes years to work through their pain." She stops and looks at the floor. "Do you remember my friend Ellie?"

"That beautiful redhead we saw at the park with her kids?"

"Jonas is her son and May is her daughter," she says with a smile. "Ellie lost her sister on the same day that May was born. She still deals with that loss. It's hard for her every year when her sister's birthday comes around."

I'd be broken if Julian died. We're not as close as we once were, but I depend on him to be there. I know he feels the same way about me.

"I'm sorry for her loss."

"I'm sorry for your loss, Brynn." Her voice softens. "I'm sorry your grandma died."

I nod my head silently as I begin to cry. "She died three years ago, Ad."

She taps her index finger on my chest. "Your heart doesn't care about that. It still misses her. It's still angry that she died."

I am still angry. I saw my grandma the day before she died. She was happy and carefree. I remember clearly the last thing she said to me was that she'd see me soon. She passed in her sleep that night from a massive heart attack.

She'd called me Jane when I left her apartment. Her full-time nurse had given me a sympathetic smile as I walked out. Alzheimer's had just taken hold of my grandma, but she was fighting back. She had more good days than bad right before her death.

"Anger is a big part of grief for many people." She looks up at the tiled ceiling before her eyes focus back on me. "I've seen family members scream at each other when they lose a pet. I've watched people tell Dr. Hunt to fuck off. I've even had people angry with me because I was in the room when Donovan told them it was time to let go."

I sit on her words for a minute, absorbing them. "Anger is a part of my grief, but I'm not mourning my Grandma Caroline anymore. I can think about her without crying."

"Crying is just a small piece of the emotional puzzle we have to put back together after we suffer a loss." She glances up at the large circular clock on the wall. "Dr. Hunt will be in soon to see Pike but I want you to think about something before you see Smith again."

"I'm seeing him tonight. I'm going over to the brownstone for dinner."

"You're going to *the* brownstone for dinner? The one he bought that you wanted?"

"Yes." I flash a weak smile. I haven't had a chance to explain to Adley about my plans for tonight yet. "I'm going to confront him about it all tonight."

"Brynn." She sighs heavily, her jaw tightening. "Do you like this guy?"

"He hurt me," I reply quickly. "I can't like him if he deliberately hurt me."

"Listen to me, carefully." She steps forward and scoops Pike into her own hands. "I think you're misdirecting the anger you feel about Caroline's death. I don't think you're pissed at Smith because he bought a house you wanted. I think you're mad as hell that Caroline died unexpectedly and you're angry with yourself because you think you let her down in some way. You're associating that with Smith because it's easier to deal with than to face what you really feel."

"No," I interrupt in a huff. "You're wrong."

"It's not his fault that she died, Brynn," she says soothingly. "So he bought a house that you wanted? Do you know how shitty you would have felt after she died being in that house all alone? It would have been pure torture for you."

I've thought about that. I always push those feelings aside and instead dwell on the small amount of time I would have had with my grandma in the house she wanted to live in. I've even tried to convince myself that her heart attack wouldn't have happened if she would have been living in the brownstone. I know it's not true, but the imagined image of her standing at the doorway with Pike in her arms waiting to go in brings me peace.

"It's a house." She enunciates each word. "It's just a house. Think long and hard about whether you're good with tossing this guy out with the trash over this because if you pin him to the wall tonight over a damn brownstone, you're going to lose any shot you have with him. You're pissed off that she's gone. Don't put that on him."

"I'm so mad that she died, Adley," I say through a sob.

"I know you are, sweetie."

What am I supposed to do with all this anger inside of me?" I almost shout, pounding my fist on my chest. "How do I make it go away?"

"You already are." She leans forward to brush her hand over my forehead. "You're talking about it to me. Keep doing that. Go see a therapist if you need to but get it all out, Brynn. Let it go. It's time."

***

Can I come over now? I know it's not six yet, but there's something I want to talk to you about.

I read my text message over once more before I finally hit send. It's just past five o'clock and I'm anxious to see Smith. It has nothing to do with the brownstone and everything to do with the conversation I had this morning with Adley.

After Dr. Hunt gave me the good news that Pike is well on the road to recovery I took him for a walk in the park by my place before I dropped him off at home.

I spent the entire afternoon with Sonya Lannen going over my rough ideas for the show suite at The Beryl. She was impressed and told me as much. I was grateful for her kind words and even more thankful that our meeting kept my mind occupied.

Adley gave me a lot to think about this morning. I want to start fresh with Smith tonight. I want to see if the kiss can lead to more.

I read his text message the second it arrives on my phone.

I'm ready if you are, Petal. Head over. I'll be here.

He doesn't know that I'm already on East Sixty-Fourth Street. I wanted to be nearby if he gave me the good-to-go. I take a deep breath, look down at the short yellow sundress and nude heels I'm wearing and I start toward the brownstone on foot.

    This is it. Tonight I'm going to do my very best to leave the past where it belongs so I can see what the future has in store for me.

Chapter 16

Smith

I worked my arms out like a motherfucker this afternoon. It wasn't at the gym. I left work shortly after noon and headed directly to Park Slope, here in Brooklyn.

A month ago I went and did the one thing I swear I'd never do again. I bought a brownstone. This one is at least in half-ass decent shape. The first one I bought three years ago was a massive pile of shit. The woman I bought it from, Sigrid Hull, did nothing to maintain it.

That's not to say that my great-grandparents did any upkeep either. By the time I got my hands on that building, it had needed a total gut job. It took me a year and a half and a small fortune to restore the place to a fraction of what it once was.

I didn't need it to be magazine worthy. I needed it be livable and wheelchair accessible.

It's one of the few brownstones on the Upper East Side that comes with an elevator. It also comes with a boatload of memories for my granddad. His family owned the building before it was sold to Sigrid's parents more than fifty years ago when my great-grandfather's business took a massive hit.

Today, I started the remodel on the home I'm going to bring my sister and her twins to. Her husband left her without a word and she wants to be in New York where her family is. I'm going to make it happen. I want them here in Brooklyn. I want to jump full force into the role of uncle to those boys.

My plan is to get Brynn on board for this project. I need her eye for design. I also want to give her a national platform to promote her business. It's the reason I've been pitching the idea to Resa of taking this remodel on air with Brynn at the helm of all the interior design aesthetics. I know we'll make a winning team.

I step out of the shower and towel-dry my hair before I look in the mirror. My left hand runs over my chest and the spot where I'm thinking of getting inked. I'm taking inspiration from Brynn's tattoo. Family is everything to me too and I'm sure as shit aware of how lucky I am in that department.

I look down at my phone on the bathroom counter when it chimes, hoping it's another message from Brynn. She texted me right before I hopped in the shower telling me she's on her way.

It's a text from my younger brother Simon.

Dude, there's a beautiful woman here looking for you.

I scratch my chin as I reread it. Then I thumb back a quick response.

I'm not falling for this again, you little shit. I have plans tonight. I can't come over.

I watch as the three small dots bounce across the screen before his reply pops up.

Gramps is telling her stories and she's eating it up. Seriously you asshole, why would a woman like this want anything to do with you?

My grandfather is talking to someone he's not related to? What the hell?

I don't have a chance to respond before his next message comes through.

Her name is Brynn. She's crying, dude. What should I do?

Brynn's at the brownstone? Why the fuck is Brynn at the brownstone?
I scoop up my phone and text a message back to him as I jog to my bedroom to get dressed.

Keep her there. I'm on my way.

***

I burst through the door of the brownstone, sweating profusely through my white T-shirt and jeans from the non-air conditioned taxi ride over. I debated taking the subway or calling on Arthur to bring me here, but a taxi, at this time of day, was the best choice to get me here as soon as possible.

I rub my hand over my brow as I scan the foyer. Nothing. Dead silence.

I call out. My voice is shaky and rough. "Brynn? Where are you?"

My sister-in-law, Jaylee, rounds the corner from the main sitting room. "Smith? What took you so long?"

"My private helicopter is in the shop," I quip. "I had to come from Brooklyn, Jay. I made good time."

"She left." She reaches out to touch my hand. "We tried to keep her here, but she took off. She was torn up about someone named Caroline. Gramps told her a few stories about this Caroline person and Brynn lost it."

"Caroline?" I search her face for another clue. "Who the hell is Caroline?"

"Someone Gramps knew when he was young."

I shake my head as I scroll through the contact list on my phone until it lands on Brynn's number. I call her but it rings straight through to voicemail.

"I don't get how she ended up here." I thumb out a quick text telling her to call me. "She told me she knew where I lived. I was waiting for her at my place."

"She knew you owned this place." She taps her bare toe on the hardwood floor. "She told Gramps that you bought it three years ago. She knew that."

How? How in the ever loving fuck does Brynn know that I bought this place? I caught wind of it when my grandpa called to tell me that Sigrid had reached out to him to give him first shot at purchasing it. The only reason she did that was because he'd stop by here on a regular basis to ask if he could sit in the garden. Sigrid's grandparents and parents never minded, but Sigrid wasn't as accommodating.

"I don't get it," I say aloud. "Where's Gramps?"

"I think he's with Simon and the boys in the kitchen." She gestures down the long, narrow corridor. "You're welcome to stay for dinner, Smith. I made enough for all of us."

"I can't stay," I mutter as I march down the corridor. "I need to find Brynn."

"Here it is." My grandfather's voice startles me from above. "I found it. I knew I'd kept it all these years."

He descends the wooden staircase slowly. He refuses to use the elevator at the back of the house. "You're just in time, my boy. I was going to show Simon and Jaylee a picture."

I move to help him, taking the steps two at a time until I reach him and plant a soft kiss on his wrinkled forehead. "Show me, Gramps. Show me the picture."

"Get me to the bottom first." He pats my hand.

I do. I lead him carefully down the stairs even though he handles them by himself multiple times a day.

"Hello to you too, Smith," my brother calls from the kitchen. "Bring that damn picture in here. We haven't had this much excitement here, well, since never."

"Don't listen to him." My grandpa holds tight to my forearm. "We play poker two nights a week after the kids go to bed. Your brother always loses to me."

I don't doubt that for a second. I've played poker with them. It brings out the best and the worst in the men in my family.

I round the corner to the kitchen and spot Simon immediately. His oldest son, Cameron, is seated next to him at the table, and his youngest, Brett, is on his lap. I lead Gramps over before I bend down and swipe my hand across Brett's brow.

"She's something else." Simon grabs my hand. "This Brynn woman is amazing."

"Hey," Jaylee laughs from behind me. "I'm right here, Simon."

"You know you're it for me, babe." He puckers his lips. "Smith's girl is perfect for us though."

"For us?" I chuckle. "What the hell does that mean?"

"She got that one to stop acting like someone pissed in his cereal." He jerks his thumb at Gramps. "Ignore the word pissed, boys."

I arch a brow. "Brynn's an incredible person."

"She colored with the boys in their coloring books, and…" his voice trails as he looks at his sons before he focuses his gaze back on my face. "She didn't ask me about the chair, Smith. Not one question. There wasn't an ounce of pity in her eyes."

I swallow back the emotion I always feel when he brings up the wheelchair he'll spend the rest of his life in. He got in a car with someone who was just as high as he was. The other guy, the driver, didn't make it when they crashed in Florida. Simon made it out with his life. He's worked hard to recover. I'm still praying for a miracle for him, even though he's embraced his life just as it is now.

Jaylee, a woman he met in rehab, has been a driving force in his recovery. They've both been clean for years and now that they're parents, they've devoted their lives to taking care of their boys and our grandfather. Simon's goal now is a teaching degree. I know he'll make it happen.

"There's no reason to pity you," I point out with a grin and a scratch to the five o'clock shadow that's settled over my jaw. "The beard you're trying to grow is pitiful but we can't all be me."

"The picture, boys." Our grandfather shoves a square, black and white photograph in the space between us. "This is Caroline."

I gaze down at the picture, my eyes locked on the young girl with the dark hair and big smile.

"Hey, this Caroline person looks just like Brynn." Simon taps his index finger on the edge of the image. "How do you know Caroline, Gramps?"

"We played together when we were kids." He runs his hand over Cameron's back. "She'd come here with her mother and we'd go in the garden. We shared our first kiss back there, if you can call it that. It wasn't more than a quick peck."

None of this makes sense to me. I've never once heard Julian mention a woman named Caroline.

"Your mom and Caroline's mom were friends?" I question.

"No." Gramps hangs his head. "Her mother worked for mine. Caroline's mom was our housekeeper. She told me she always wanted to live in this house and I told her we were like family so she should move right in. I didn't understand that's not how it worked with the help."

I lace my fingers behind my neck and take a deep breath. I need answers and there's only one person who can give them to me since Brynn has gone silent. I type out a text to Julian and then press send.

I need you to tell me who Caroline is. I'm looking at a picture of her from when she was a kid. She looks just like Brynn.

"Soon after this picture was taken your great grandmother fired her mother and I never saw

Caroline again. I tried to find her after your grandmother died, but I couldn't track her down."

I drop my gaze back to my phone when it chimes, my heart hammering in my chest as I read Julian's text.

A picture? Of Caroline? Where are you? What the hell is going on?

I don't have time to get into the long version of this twisted tale. I want a short and sweet answer so I can understand why Brynn is so torn up.

Who is Caroline?

I send it off as my grandfather starts off on a tangent about when he was a kid. His words all blend together as I stare at my phone.

Our grandmother. Jane's mother. She died a couple of years ago. I barely knew her.

"Would you look at this?" Gramps waves the picture in the air again, this time the back is visible. "Caroline drew a little something for me here. I forgot all about that."

I snatch the picture from his hand and stare at the faded pencil drawing. It's a heart with one word written inside of it. Family.

It's an exact match to the tattoo on Brynn's elbow.

Another text message pops up on my phone from Julian.

She was Brynn's whole world. I don't think she's ever gotten over her death. It broke her. She hasn't been the same since.

There's only one place Brynn runs to when she's broken. I know where and as I take off down the long corridor toward the front door of the brownstone, I yell back at my family that I love them. I do, but not as much as I love my beautiful Brynn.

Chapter 17

Brynn

I swing open the rooftop door to find him there. I knew the second I heard the soft raps at the door that it would be Smith. I'd come straight to the top of the world from the brownstone.

"You've been crying." He reaches for my face with both hands and cups it. "Jesus, Brynn. This is all fucked up."

It is. When I knocked at the door of the brownstone, I fully expected Smith to answer. I was shocked when a tall woman with a long blond braid greeted me. She knew Smith she said, but he didn't live there. He lives in Brooklyn she told me before she pulled me into the house and introduced me to his family.

I met his brother, his nephews and finally, I met, Gramps, his handsome grandfather.

Gramps sat silently in a chair and watched me as I talked to Smith's brother and nephews. Out of nowhere, his granddad blurted out that I looked like Caroline.

My heart stopped for a full two beats at that moment.

He moved to sit next to me then and told me stories about when they were both children in the house. He'd push her on the swing that used to hang from a tree out back; a tree that was chopped down at some point and replaced with a fountain and a statue of a dog.

He showed me the garden and the kitchen where my grandma used to sit on the floor and draw.

Then he pointed out the pantry and the script of her name that is still barely visible on the door.

Smith bought that home for his family so his grandpa could enjoy the memories he made there and so his brother, his wife and their sons could create a life there for themselves.

"My grandma knew your grandpa," I say through a small sob. "You bought the house for him. I wanted to buy it for her."

"You wanted to buy the house?" He ushers me across the roof to where the two chairs are. "Do you want to sit?"

"No." I shake my head. "I mean yes. I wanted to buy the house. I don't want to sit."

"We need to back up." He reaches for both of my hands and I let him. I don't pull away because I need the comfort. I've been aching for it since I left the brownstone. "Why did you go there, Brynn? What made you think I live there?"

I don't know which direction to head with this. I can tell him that I saw him outside when I was semi-stalking the place or I can tell him I made a broker break his code of ethics by telling me that Smith was the person who bought the brownstone. I decide to tell him the truth. "I did see you on the street with groceries the other day. I was on the sidewalk across from the brownstone. Also, three years ago I asked someone to check who bought the place when Sigrid put it up for sale. I know it was you."

He takes a measured step back but his hands don't leave mine. "Do you know Sigrid?"

Would it matter at this point if I did? I don't give a shit that the two of them were likely sharing an expensive bottle of champagne along with a great fuck to celebrate Smith closing on her brownstone. I do give two shits about the fact that my life feels like it just fell off the edge of the earth and I'm coasting through the universe with nothing to ground me right now. "No. I never met her. I got her name from the agent I used to help me place my offer."

"Your offer?"

I pull my hands from his to scrub the back of my neck with my fingers. "The offer I put in for the brownstone, Smith. That's how I knew who Sigrid was. That's also why I called you twice asking you to put in a good word for me with her so she would accept my offer. I wanted to live in that house with my grandma. It was her dream. She told me she spent the happiest moments of her life in that house."

He stumbles back until his heels hit the edge of one of the chairs. He lowers himself down into the seat. "What the hell? What?"

"What the hell about what?" I parrot back. "You already know all of this."

He rests both of his elbows on his thighs, his head hanging down. "I know none of this, Brynn. None of it. I had no idea you wanted that place. I never got a call from you. You and I only spoke on the phone once, and that was when you were at Easton Pub and I came to get you."

Technically, that's true. "I left you two voicemail messages about Sigrid's place. I never heard back."

He looks down at the phone in his hand. "You called what number?"

"Your number," I say exasperated.

"Julian gave you my number?" He waves his phone in the air.

"No." I swallow past the lump in my throat. "I wanted to buy the house on my own and surprise my family, so I didn't ask for any of their help, not even Julian's. I called your office in Los Angeles. You were doing that Hollywood gossip show then."

A grin peaks the corners of his mouth. "It was an entertainment newsmagazine."

I don't want to love that smile as much as I do right now but my heart won't let me hate it anymore, or him. "You didn't get my messages, did you?"

"Not a one." He taps his phone against the arm of the chair. "My assistant screened all my calls. She had hundreds a day to run through. A lot of them were from women wanting to talk directly to me so I gave her carte blanche to delete everything she didn't think was worth my time."

That explains that.

"You said you put an offer in on the brownstone?" His jaw tightens. "Sigrid told me that mine was the only one on the table."

Since we're putting everything out there, I take it an extra step. "My offer was full ask, cash, a thirty day close and no contingencies."

My eyes wander to the view of the Brooklyn Bridge. It's no wonder he was staring in that direction the other night. It's the place he now calls home.

"All cash and no contingencies? My offer was shit compared to that."

"I know," I blurt out without thinking.

"You know?" He lifts his brows and tilts his head.

"I went all in against the advice of my broker. I assume your broker wouldn't let you do that." I try to correct with a small smile.

"Either Sigrid is an idiot or something doesn't add up." He swipes his finger over his phone's screen. "If you want me to find out why she took my offer, let me know and I can make the call."

"We both know why she took your offer." I shrug. "It doesn't matter at this point, Smith. Your family is happy there. I have a great apartment and the past is in the past."

"Slow down." He stands and stalks back toward me. "I don't know why she took my offer so explain that to me."

"You know why." My eyes drop to the concrete. "You two were in a relationship."

I feel his finger brush against my chin. "Look at me."

I do. I don't want to but I do.

"Sigrid's family bought the house from my great grandparents so she called my Gramps and told him the brownstone was his if he had the money. He didn't so I flew here, hammered out a deal with her and the rest is history."

"You hammered out a deal with her?" I cross my arms. "Is that a polite way of saying you slept with her to get the deal done?"

He throws his head back in laughter. "You're jealous. You think my cock is worth more than a full ask, all cash deal? I mean I think it is, but I'm fucking over the moon to know that you do too and you haven't even seen me naked yet."

Yet.

I bite my bottom lip. It sounds ridiculous when put like that. "You took her to the Met Gala."

"I had pants on." He pats his thigh. "I always had my pants on with her. My broker fought hard for the deal I got and it was nowhere close to what you were offering. Maybe Sigrid had a soft spot for Gramps or maybe she wanted the building to go back to my family. I have no fucking clue but I can find out if it means you'll stop hating me."

I just want this to be over. I'm tired of beating myself up over a house this is now home to a wonderful group of people. Whatever magic lived there when my grandma met his grandfather isn't there anymore. At least, it's not for me. My magic is the feeling in my chest. It's my heart opening up to this man in front of me.

"I don't hate you." I look into his intensely dark eyes. "I haven't handled my grandma's death very well. I needed someone to direct all my anger at."

"I'm your guy." He crosses his arms over his chest. "I get how much that hurts, Petal. I lost my grandma too. It split me in two."

"I want to be put back together," I whisper. "Can we go to Brooklyn?"

"Only if you let me kiss you when we get there." He brushes the pad of his thumb over my bottom lip.

"I'll let you do more."

"What the fuck are we doing up here?" His hand reaches for mine. "Let's go."

Chapter 18

Smith

You never know what's around the corner. I thought I'd be cooking Brynn my world famous spaghetti Bolognese tonight. I can claim that title because I cooked it on the show two weeks ago and the recipe was downloaded more than a million times.

Boom. Take that Tyler Monroe, big shot Manhattan chef.

We're in my apartment now, but the only thing on fire is my cock. I'm seriously rocking the world's most sensitive hard-on right now. I haven't even undressed and I'm about to blow my load.

"I feel sweaty." She runs her slender fingers over her forearm. "It's so muggy outside tonight."

Damn right it is. My shirt is a testament to that. The thing is glued to my chest and back. I could go for another shower right about now.

"Let's take a shower," I suggest because I need it, preferably on the cold side so my dick can take a step back and calm down before I embarrass myself.

"You go first," she says in that sweet voice of hers.

Her voice is even getting to me right now. I feel like a teenage kid who just got his first flash of a naked tit. She's still fully clothed, so God help me when I finally see what's under that yellow dress she's wearing.

"Together," I counter. "You and me in the shower now, Petal."

Her hands jump to her stomach. "That seems like a bad idea to me."

"I promise to close my eyes." I give her a wink. "For the first ten seconds."

She tosses me a look that either says fuck off or fuck me. I'm going with the latter because it's all I want right now. The throbbing in my dick has now trailed down my thighs. I think this woman is literally going to bring me to my knees in the next twenty seconds if I don't see her bare flesh.

Her hand brushes over her face, pushing a strand of her hair back. "I'm nervous. I haven't been naked in front of a lot of men."

One is too many for me to comprehend right now. I want this all to myself. I want her to be mine; tonight, tomorrow and for every damn day I draw a breath.

"I'll hit the shower first," I offer with a kiss to her hand. "You come in when you're ready. If you want to go after I'm done, I'm good with that too. No pressure."

She nods, drawing her bottom lip between her teeth.

Shit. I think I might come from the sight of that.

"Make yourself at home." I motion with my chin toward the kitchen. "Help yourself to whatever's in the fridge if you get thirsty."

She doesn't say anything as I walk backward down the hallway that leads to my bathroom, my eyes still glued to her. "I'm glad you're here."

"I am too," she calls after me just as I drop my shirt on the floor and head to the shower.

***

I scrub my hands over my face one last time. I have no idea how long I've been in here, but time is running out. If Petal was going to make an appearance, I think that would have happened by now.

I should shut off the water, towel-dry and hunt her down. I want to but I'm scared shitless that when I step back into the other room, that she'll be gone. A lot has gone down tonight and I wouldn't blame her if she needed a day or two to take it all in.

I push my head back under the spray, the sound of the water drowning out everything else.

Then I feel it.

It's faint at first and I can't tell if it's my motherfucking mind playing tempting tricks on me or not. I want it to be her. I want to spin around and see a wet, naked and willing Brynn Bishop staring back at me.

"Don't turn around," she whispers in my ear. "Not yet."

I nod as I reach down to grab hold of her hand and press it against my rock hard abs. I know how much she's wanted to touch me. I've watched her watching me in the gym.

"I like my body."

"You should," I say as I bend my neck back. "It's the most beautiful body I've ever seen."

"You haven't seen it yet, Smith."

I pull her hand up with mine and kiss her palm; softly, sweetly and exactly the way I'm going to kiss the inside of her thigh before I devour her pussy within the next ten minutes.

"I see it in my dreams every night, Petal."

She sighs and then chuckles. "You don't have to use those lines on me, Smith. I don't want you to."

I pivot so quickly that she doesn't realize what's happening until I'm staring at her beautiful, flawless face. I don't drop my eyes because I'm going to wait until she's ready for me to soak in her perfection. "I'll never bullshit you. Never. I dream about you. I have almost every night since I saw you at the gym."

Her lips twist together in a way that I wish my dick was a part of, but it's not. It's bouncing against my stomach, hard and aching for me to acknowledge that it still exists.

"Are you being real right now?"

I cup her face in my hands as the water beats a warm path over my back. "I have wanted you for a long time. I wanted you that night when you were seventeen, Brynn, but I didn't take the chance. I was too chicken shit to do it and that haunted me for a long time."

Her gaze drops. I know she's taking in my body. "I've never been with a man like you before."

"Like me?" I question because this is a one shot deal. I get to hear her first impression of my body this one time and I want to remember every single word of it since I have no intention of ever showing this to another woman again.

"Every part of you is so hard and strong." Her hands run over my chest. "It's not just your chest or your abs or every other part. It's all of it. Even your heart is strong."

"Can I look at you now?"

Her head pops back up. "You haven't looked yet?"

I see a flash of panic over her expression. I don't know why she's worried. I already know that I'm in the presence of something I've never experienced before. I haven't felt anything even close to this with another woman.

I let my eyes slide down her face to her neck before I take in her breasts. They're plump and round, her nipples a pale shade of pink. The rest of her is just as magnificent. Smooth skin and a small strip of trimmed dark hair that leads to what I'm craving right now more than anything.

"Can I touch you?" I whisper into the air between us. "I want to feel you come on my fingers."

Her cheeks are pink but I can't tell if she's blushing or if it's from the warmth of the water. "Please."

That's all I need. I wrap my arm around her waist, pull her close to me and kiss her mouth exactly the way I want to kiss the rest of her.

Chapter 19

Brynn

I think I came apart in less than a minute. Smith touched me in a way I've never been touched before, even by myself. I didn't stop him when his hand slid down my belly and he tapped me on each thigh. He wanted me to part my legs for him, so I did. I leaned back on the shower wall, grabbed hold of his shoulders and let him use his fingers to bring me to an orgasm.

Although, for the record, there should be a word that describes an orgasm that is better than the best.

A moregasm is what I'm going to call it and Smith Booth is the man who invented it.

"You're beautiful when you come, Brynn." He pulls me closer to him. We're in his bed now. He took me by the hand and brought me here after I came in the shower. I didn't think my legs would hold me up but they did.

I like that he thinks so. I have no idea what my face looks like when it happens. All I know is that if he hadn't been there to hold me up, I would have crashed to the shower floor in a puddle of pure mush.

I reach down to touch the tip of his cock. It's still hard. It's still just as large as it was when I first saw it in the shower. It has to be at least nine inches, thick and heavily veined. "Can I taste it?"

He pushes the sheet that's covering us both down revealing his erection. "I can't promise that I won't come as soon as your lips touch me, but I'm willing to risk it."

I haven't given more than a half dozen blowjobs total in my life. It's intimate. In many ways, to me, it feels more intimate than actual fucking. I want it though. I've been daydreaming about wrapping my lips around it since I saw it in the shower.

I scoot down the bed and press a soft kiss to his stomach before I wrap my hand around him. My fingers don't quite touch my thumb. Seeing that sends a jolt of heat to my core. I know it's going to burn when he's inside me. "I like it."

"You like it?" He chuckles. "Thank fuck because it's all I have to work with."

I look up at his face. He's so handsome, much more handsome than he was eight years ago. He's grown into himself. He's comfortable and content, and right now, he's all mine.

I lick the tip of his cock gently, savoring the salty taste of his flesh. It rocks in my hand, an angry signal that he's beyond the point of arousal. He's primed for a fuck. I am too, but I want this to last. I don't know what's going to happen tomorrow and if this is my only taste of him, I want to enjoy every second of this.

"Suck it, Petal. I need it."

I moan softly as I close my mouth over it and slide my lips down. I push back my body's urge to stop. I go past that. I feel him harden even more when the tip barely brushes the back of my throat.

"Goddammit," he grits out in a low, rough and sexy-as-sin tone. "If I blow this down your pretty little throat, forgive me, but it's too good. It's just too fucking good."

I suck harder, my head moving up and down with his hands tangled in my hair to guide me. His hips rock, my hands glide; the pace frantic and then relaxed and I when I hear the low growl from deep inside of him and sense his balls tighten, I firm my grip.

"This. Is. It." He tugs on my hair to pull me up, but I shake it off.

I won't move. I need this. I have to have it.

"Dammit, Brynn. For fuck's sake," he groans as he shoots his release and I take it all.

***

"You didn't think you would make it out of here without feeling my cock inside that tight pussy, did you?"

If this is a dream, please never let me wake up.

My eyes pop open and adjust to the minimal light in the room. I fell asleep after I blew him. I fucking fell asleep. Isn't the man the one who is supposed to lull himself into dreamland after he comes?

I roll over quickly until I'm facing him. His hair is mussed, the brush of whiskers covering his jaw are thicker than they were earlier and he's staring at me like he's going to eat me alive.

Not that I would complain about that. I've imagined his tongue on my pussy for years. I have no doubt that reality is going to trump every single one of those daydreams.

"You have to get up soon." I motion past his shoulder to the digital clock blinking a blue display of the time. It's after midnight now.

I didn't just take a nap. I fucking hibernated in his bed.

"I have to fuck you soon." He rips open a condom package that he pulled out of thin air.

I watch closely as he rolls onto his back and sheaths his thick cock. It's hard again. This man is a beast.

He taps my thigh with his fingers. "I want a taste. Get over here."

I've only ever been on my back when a man has eaten me out. I've never been on top.

"Please, Petal." He slicks his bottom lip with his tongue. "I'm dying here."

I scoot up until I'm straddling his stomach, his cock bouncing against my ass cheek. "You want to taste me?"

He runs his large hands over my thighs. "That's what I said."

I'm not going to argue with the man. Instead, I slide up his body until I'm hovering over his mouth. He yanks me down and grazes his tongue along the seam of my pussy.

I moan because it's just too fucking good to keep everything inside when it feels like this.

When he sucks on my clit, I bow my back and tense my thighs. He breathes against my flesh, the sensation pulling even more to the surface. He groans and moans in concert with the noises issuing from my own body. I can't control the sounds I'm making because it feels too damn good to stop any of it.

It doesn't take long for me to feel that shiver race over my spine. It's the same sensation I felt earlier when his fingers were inside me.

I clench around his tongue as I feel the wave hit me with the force of a hurricane. I grab hold of the headboard, grinding down and onto his tongue, taking, using and making sure that he never forgets my taste.

He has me on my back before I can wrap my brain around what's happening. My legs move involuntarily as I ride out the crest of pleasure. He urges them apart with his own and before my climax has quieted, he pushes me into another with his cock as he buries himself inside of me in one single solid thrust.

I open my mouth to scream but there's nothing there. It's just air and then the scent of his skin surrounds me and I hear it. It's the sound of the hiss of my name as it comes off his lips.

"I'm going to…oh God, I'm going to…" my voice trails as I spit out the words, breathlessly, like a chant.

"Do it," his voice is a delicious combination of dark and rough. "Come again so I can fuck you the way I really want."

The promise of that sends me straight into an orgasm more intense than the two – or is it three- that I've already had tonight. I beat his shoulders with my fists, angry at him for making me feel this good and pissed as hell that he can take me to this place so fast that it doesn't last forever.

He slides his hand under my ass, dragging his palm along my skin until he raises my leg so my ankle rests on his shoulder. "I can't promise this won't hurt, Petal, but I need to be deeper. I want you to feel me for the next week."

"I'll feel you forever," I say softly as I tug him closer so I can kiss his mouth. "Use me, Smith. Make me feel it all."

He does. He fucks me hard, not once, but twice before I fall fast asleep again.

Chapter 20

Smith

I left her in my bed. It was the hardest thing I've ever done in my life, but I need this job. I love this job, and I know when I'm on air today, I'm going to have the biggest fucking grin on my face, even when I'm interviewing the sorry shit who just wrote a tell-all about his time with one of the most influential women in Hollywood.

You never sell out a woman you've fucked, dude. That's going to be my off the record advice for the douche.

I even gave Arthur a pat on the shoulder today when he opened the car door and handed me a steaming hot cup of Roasting Point's premium blend. The look of confusion on his face said it all. I'm not the nicest guy first thing in the morning. We both know it.

I plug my phone into my laptop as I settle in. The battery died sometime between my impromptu visit with Gramps and this morning. Normally, I'd be in full panic mode about the calls, emails and text messages I missed, but not today. Nothing on earth could have taken me away from Brynn last night.

My phone lights up like a goddamn Christmas tree. I scroll through the text messages, all from the same person. Julian.

Where the hell are you?

You can't just drop a bombshell like that on me and then vanish.
She's my sister, you asshole.
Is she all right? Tell me she's all right.

I type out a quick text in response even though I know he's fast asleep. The last text message he sent me is time stamped three hours ago.

She's fine, Julian. I've got her.

I drop my phone in my lap and take a long sip of coffee. I haven't felt this good in years, maybe ever.

I jump when I hear the chime of my phone. I drop my gaze.

You're in love with her, aren't you?

Surprise, surprise. Brynn's brother is wide awake.

I text back a response. It's short, sweet and sums everything in one word.

Yes.

Those three little dots jump on the screen as he types back a response. I don't give a shit if he has a problem with this or not. Brynn is all grown-up and what happened last night is just the beginning.

It's about time you realized it.

I laugh so hard that Arthur tips back his chin to look at me in the rear view mirror.

What the fuck does that mean? I press send.

"Is everything all right, sir?" Arthur asks, his eyes darting between the mirror and the road.

"Couldn't be better." I toss him a wink.

I was in the doorway of the kitchen that night. I saw her try to kiss you. I know it killed you inside not to.

Who the fuck knew Julian was so stealthy? I don't think twice before I thumb out a response.

I couldn't touch her back then. She was young and I didn't want you to beat the shit out of me.

At least two minutes pass before my phone chimes again.

She's an adult now but rest assured, if you hurt her, I'll beat the shit out of you now.

I laugh again. I wasn't worried either way if Julian was good with this or not, but knowing he is, does bring a sigh of relief from within.

I love you too.

I press send, slide my phone aside and open my email app on my laptop to read the notes Resa sent me thirty minutes ago. My day is about to begin and knowing that Brynn is tucked in my bed dreaming about everything we did last night makes me the happiest man on earth.

***

"You met Mavis?" I reach across the table to scoop Brynn's hand into mine. "When did that happen?"

She looks around the crowded café. It was her idea to meet here. I wanted to take her back to my bed, but she's got a meeting with a big shot developer and a contractor in an hour so I need to squeeze every second I can out of this coffee date.

"I was leaving your place. She said hi in the corridor." She tugs her hand away and pats her purse.

"Thank you for leaving me a key so I could lock up. I'll give it back to you now."

I did leave her a key. I needed her to secure the deadbolt of my apartment door when she left. It's not that I don't trust every single soul who lives in my building. I do. I don't trust the people who wander in from the street.

"I'd like you to keep it."

Her hands stop just as she's pulling on the silver chain that the key to the rooftop deck is attached to. "You want me to keep it?"

My eyes follow her movements as she tugs the remainder of the chain free. I see two keys now. One has to be my apartment key. I want it to stay there. I know it's early for that, but my heart is telling me this is it for me, so fuck conventional wisdom that says you don't give a key to a woman until you've dated for a few months.

"Yes," I say quietly. "Does that make you uncomfortable?"

She exhales softly. "Is it too soon for that? I can't give you a key to my apartment because I have a roommate and most of the time she doesn't have clothes on."

I don't give a shit about that. There's only one woman I want to see naked and she's looking right at me. "We can hang out at my place and if you have a key it makes it easier. I leave for work in the middle of the night, Brynn. You can sleep in when you stay over and lock up like you did today.

She scratches her brow. "That does make sense."

"Keep it. I want you to."

As I watch her tuck the chain back into her purse, a silver ring with a small diamond setting falls out. It bounces once on the table before it lands on the floor. I'm on my knees in an instant, chasing after it as it rolls under our table.

"Oh no, no," Brynn mutters as she drops to her knees next to me. "I can't lose that. Please, Smith. Don't let me lose it."

I won't. I have no idea why it means so much to her, but I'm not about to let it slip away. I crawl another foot forward until I slap my hand down on it, blocking the path of a couple ready to leave the café.

"Hey, you're Smith Booth, aren't you?" The woman crouches, her skirt shifting so I can literally see right up her dress.

I scramble to my feet, brushing the knees of my pants to get rid of the dirt that's settled there. I'm still wearing the suit I was earlier when I was on air. It's just past noon now, and normally I'd be in meetings discussing tomorrow's show. I ducked out to see Brynn.

"Can I get your autograph?" She's on her feet now too; her hand fishing inside her bag for what I assume is a pen.

I look down at the ring in my hand before I turn back to find Brynn standing behind me, a broad smile on her face. "He'd be more than happy to give you an autograph."

The woman taps me on the shoulder before she shoves a pen and what looks like a take-out menu from a pizza restaurant at me. "Make it out to Bonnie, with a B."

Is there another way to spell Bonnie that doesn't begin with a B?

"Are you his wife?" Bonnie, with a capital B, asks Brynn.

Brynn stammers through a series of "I…no…we used to be friends…not really, but then last night everything changed."

"She will be," I interrupt. "I'm going to marry this woman one day."

"Smith," Brynn says breathlessly as her hand lands on my shoulder. "You don't know that."

I hand Bonnie back her pen and the menu that now has my signature scribbled across it. Then I turn to my love. "Is this your grandmother's ring, Brynn?"

Her eyes drop to my open palm at the ring that I'm still holding. "It was originally my great-grandma's wedding ring. She left it to my grandma and she left it to me. My grandma told me her parents had a very special love."

"On the day you tell me you want to marry me, I'll slip it on your finger."

She leans forward, her eyes wide and open. "You're saying these things because we had great sex last night."

"I'm saying these things because I'm in love with you," I whisper against the shell of her ear.

"You can't be serious?" She steps back and scans my face. "How can you be in love with me?"

"Ask my heart." I tap my fingers against the center of my chest. "I've never been in love before and my Gramps told me that when it happened, I'd know, so I know."

Tears glisten in the corner of those brilliant blue eyes. "You know I loved you when I was seventeen, right?"

"And every day since," I add with a soft kiss to her mouth.

"I hated you yesterday when I woke up. I can't love you now." She shrugs through a half-grin. "I don't think that's how love works."

"I know it works that way." I open my palm again. "I'm going to give this back to you now, Brynn, because I know you won't let me keep it. One day I'll put it on your finger forever."

I place the ring in her hand, fist mine around it and hold it to my chest.

"You're as confusing now as you were when I was seventeen." She leans into me. "Kiss me, Smith. Just kiss me."

I do.

Chapter 21

Brynn

I can't be in love with Smith Booth, can I? We had mind-blowing, toe-curling sex and then he told me he loves me.

He looks at me in a way that Joel never did. He makes me feel things that I didn't know were possible. I can't just blurt out those three words to a man I've spent most of my adult life hating-from-afar.

I try and shake off the conversation I just had with Smith at the café and focus on the task at hand.

I'm in a meeting with Sonya Lannen, her assistant and the contractor who I'll be working side-by-side with to complete the show suite at The Beryl.

"I'm just going to say this, Brynn because I feel it's important to get it out there."

I wouldn't be able to read this woman's face if my life depended on it. She's as reserved as they come which isn't surprising. She's a part of Manhattan's elite. Technically, I am too, since I'm a Bishop, but I don't celebrate that the way the Lennans do even though my net worth is likely double theirs.

I was gifted with two trust funds in the first twenty-four years of my life. One that my parents had set up for me when I was a baby, the other comprised completely of my grandmother's estate. She may have started in life on meager means, but she inherited her wealth from my late grandfather.

My mother was her only child and when they argued because my grandma didn't want to move in with my parents, my grandma turned to me for comfort.

She treated me like I was the center of her universe. She believed in me and when she started to slip into the hands of her Alzheimer's my face morphed into my mother's in her mind, and my grandma said all the things she wished she would have when my mom was young.

I was the tie that reconnected the two of them the last year of my grandma's life.

"Are you listening, Brynn?" Sonya brushes her hand over my bare forearm. I dressed up for this meeting, even though it's the middle of August. I'm wearing a black sleeveless dress, my hair is down and straight and my make-up is on point.

"I am," I answer quickly. "I was just thinking about the wood for the master closet. We're having that imported from Borneo. I'll have a sample to show you tomorrow."

It's a great save if I do say so myself.

"Good. I'm anxious to see it." She leans back in her leather chair. We're in a conference room at the main offices of The Lennan Group NYC. "I didn't know what to expect when I found out it was you who landed this job. This is the exact point I wanted to touch on."

I don't follow and my raised brows say as much.

"I'd appreciate if you didn't talk shop with your father."

I skim my tongue over my top teeth. It shouldn't bother me as much as it does when someone brings up my dad. I get it. He's a big deal in Manhattan real estate and when a developer is working on something of this magnitude they want to keep it under wraps until they're ready to choose the broker they want to work with.

"I make it a point to never discuss business with him," I answer politely.

"Even this project?" She leans forward until her elbows are on the conference table. She's dressed all in white like an angel but this woman is far from that. She's ruthless. I've seen it myself these past few weeks as I've listened to her berate employees over the phone and push contractors into the corner over the smallest details.

"Any project I work on."

"Your father isn't the broker on any of your other projects, is he?"

I don't drop my mask. I keep it in place even though my lower jaw is about to fall into my lap.

"You did know that you were hired as part of his deal with us, right?" She practically sings the words out. Her voice raises an octave or two.

I nod, because I can't form even a single word in response.

"He wanted a say in the design elements, we didn't agree with those terms so he suggested we hire you. I fought against it Brynn, but when my father saw what you'd done to your apartment, he was on board with the idea."

Cooper made it seem as if I landed this job strictly on my own merit.

"I'm not an idiot. I know that Fulton will try and influence the project using you as his mule, but I can't let that happen."

His mule? Seriously? My father rarely even talks to me.

"He thinks he knows the needs and tastes of our future clients better than we do. If it was up to me, I'd hire a younger broker, but Cooper insisted on Fulton. He's locked into this and so are you now, so let me be crystal clear."

I don't even blink an eye as I listen.

"Do not show your father any samples. Don't bring his ridiculous old-school ideas to me and try to sell them. I'll know it's coming from him and if it happens, I'll make damn sure that every other developer in this city is aware that hiring you is a big mistake."

"Understood." I snap open the leather portfolio in front of me. "I have a list of finishes I want to go over for the main bathroom. I'm ready if you are."

***

I watch him as he crosses Madison Avenue. He moves fluidly, like a shark in the ocean. That's who he is in this city. His black hair is now a peppered shade of gray, his blue eyes have always been darker than mine, but his smile is the same as it was when I was a little girl begging for his attention.

"Daddy," I call out to him with a wave of my hand.

He spots me immediately, a genuine smile taking over his handsome face. "Bernie, it's you."

Bernie.

The nickname he gave me in middle school when I burned a slice of bread every day for an entire week before I realized that there was a setting on the toaster that controlled the time.

"I need to talk to you," I say as I feel his arms circle me. He pulls me into a tight hug. I breathe in the scent of his cologne. It's the same cologne he's worn every day for my entire life.

His lips brush over my forehead. "You're more beautiful every time I see you. How is that possible?"

I think I'm in love, Daddy. He makes me feel more beautiful than I ever have felt before.

That's what I want to say but I don't. We've never discussed any of my relationships before. The only time he voiced an opinion on my personal life is when he told me he thought I'd regret ending things with Joel. He was wrong.

"Come up to my office." He gestures to the large building we're in front of. I arrived just moments before he did and when I looked back to the street, I saw him. Tall, debonair and drawing the attention of people in every direction.

At one time he was my hero. That's not the case anymore.

I follow his lead and let him guide me through the lobby and into the elevator of the skyscraper. He doesn't say a word as his eyes scan his phone and his fingers tap out messages to people who will undoubtedly pad his bank account.

His firm employs more than three hundred brokers who work in all five boroughs. His business is his life. It always has been and I suspect it always will be.

We pass his assistant, a handsome man with a beard, who calls out my name as if we've met. We haven't. He recognizes me from the picture that was taken at my graduation of me and my parents. One almost identical, but with my brother's smiling face while he's wearing his cap and gown, hangs next to it in my dad's private office.

"Do you want anything?" My dad shrugs off his suit jacket and hangs it on a coat rack near the door before he closes it behind us. "I remember you liked tea. I can get you an iced tea, Bern. Would you like that?"

He's trying and that's more than he usually does. He may have attempted to call me twice in the past two weeks but that pales in comparison to the two calls a day I was making to him after my grandma died. He rarely picked up. He was always in a meeting or out at a showing. I was never at the top of his priority list, the way he was on mine.

"I'm fine," I say as I sit on a leather couch next to a bank of windows. "I'm sorry I missed your calls. I tried calling you back but you must have been busy."

He sits next to me, crossing his legs at the knees. "Business is good. I'm taking on new listings every day."

Of course, he is. He's in an ongoing competition with himself to prove that he still has it.

He looks down at the expensive watch on his wrist. "I have a showing in an hour but I'm glad you stopped by. I know what it's about."

I scan the pictures hung on the wall next to those of my brother and me. Many of them are famous faces; clients that he helped to either buy or sell their property. There's one of him and the mayor and another of him with my mother in Hawaii. It must have been taken more than twenty years ago. I can't remember the last time he ventured out of New York.

"You're here about The Beryl aren't you?" His voice softens as my gaze travels over another photograph. "I didn't push for you to come on board for any reason other than I believe strongly that you're the most qualified person for the job."

I stand and walk over to the wall of pictures. I walk past them all as he talks about Cooper and friendship and commitment to a bigger picture.

My ears start to ring as I stand in front of the image of my father, dressed in a tuxedo, my mother standing next to him and three other people, all smiling brightly for the camera.

I hear him behind me and his footsteps on the hardwood as he nears where I am.

I raise my finger to the frame and tap the edge. "Is this from the Met Gala?"

"It is." He wraps his arm around my shoulder. "Wasn't your mom a vision in that dress? I had it tailored made for her."

"That's Smith Booth." I touch my finger to the glass.

He nods. "That's right, and that's Sigrid Hull, one of the most beautiful women I've ever met."

"Who is that next to her?" I turn to look at my dad, waiting for the answer I already know.

"Otto Schmidt. He's one of my top agents."

I study his face, waiting for the smile to break, but it doesn't. "How long has he worked for you?"

I see the moment it happens. His expression shifts. Panic washes over his face as realization hits him like a ton of bricks. "I hired him the night of the Gala."

"What did you do?" I grab hold of his forearm and shake. "It was you, wasn't it? Tell me what you did."

"Bernie." His voice cracks as he turns to look at me. "That brownstone was a money pit. You would have regretted that decision for the rest of your life."

"What did you do?" I repeat my question, desperate for an answer.

"He wanted a job. Otto wanted a job with the firm." He rakes both hands through his hair. "He came to me with your offer because he felt it wasn't prudent. He thought you were making a mistake going in so aggressively. I told him I'd take care of it."

"He was legally obligated to present that offer." I firm my stance, crossing my arms over my chest. "He had to present my offer."

"It wasn't in your best interest to go in with that offer."

"Sigrid never saw my offer?" I scrub my hand over my forehead. "Are you saying she never saw it?"

He stands in silence. His eyes are focused clearly on mine.

"Answer me," I snap. "Are you the reason I never got to buy that place for grandma?"

"Yes," he whispers. "I'm the reason."

I shake my head. "That and now The Beryl. Why, daddy? Why control my life like this?"

His knuckles pop as he fists his right hand. "You stopped needing me. Somewhere along the way you just stopped needing me."

Tears well in the corners of my eyes. "I've never stopped needing you. You stopped needing me, Daddy. You shut me out. I've been nothing to you for a long time."

"No," he shouts the word out, his voice cracking. "You are everything to me. You and Julian."

"When is my birthday?"

His brow furrows as he thinks.

"You don't know, do you?" I bite back. "Why did I break up with Joel?"

"Bernie, please," he pleads. "I've tried my best. I wanted to make a good life for you and your brother. You wouldn't have the apartment you do now if it wasn't for me."

"None of that matters to me." I swipe my hand over my face. "Family matters to me. It has always mattered to me and I feel like I don't have one."

"You have a family," he huffs out the words in a laugh. "We are your family."

"Start acting like it." I brush past him. "When you can act like the father I need, call me."

Chapter 22

Smith

"Fulton is a crafty bastard," I say as I wrap my arms around Brynn. "Can't he get in deep shit for manipulating the sale of the brownstone?"

She nods as she looks up at my face. "Very deep shit but it would mean contacting Sigrid to tell her that she lost out on a better sale."

"You know my offer was like twenty-five grand less than your offer, right?"

"Only twenty-five thousand?" Her eyes widen. "I thought it was a lot lower than that."

"The intel your spy was feeding you was off base then." I chuckle. "I wanted that place for Gramps, so I went in with a solid offer."

"I'm glad he's there and your brother and sister-in-law too."

"I'm glad you're here." I move my hand along her bare leg. We're naked, as expected. We ate dinner in the nude in the dining room and then I brought her to bed. I haven't touched her yet. I could tell she wanted to talk.

"I hated you for no reason for a long time." Her smile fades. "Jesus, Smith. I literally couldn't stand to think about you and it was all over a piece of property. How fucked up is that?"

"First let me say," I begin, as I move my hand between her legs. "It's going to take me some time to get used to the fact that you say the word *fuck*. It makes my cock hard-as-steel when you do it."

She glides her hand down my stomach until it brushes the tip of my dick. "I see what you mean and fuck, fuckery, fuck fuck a dee."

I moan. "Your mouth is going to kill me."

"My mouth will take care of your hard-as-steel cock in a minute."

"Another word I've never heard you say."

"Minute?" She kisses my cheek. "Is that it?"

"Try again," I slide my finger over her clit.

She whimpers as her legs part further. "Mouth?"

I twirl the tip of my thumb over her entrance. "If you miss it a third time, I'll make you come using your own hand."

She presses her fingers over mine. "Cock, I said cock. Cock a doodle… Oh, fuck, Smith. Right there."

I want more. I'm always going to want more of this. "Keep talking, baby."

"I can't talk when you touch me like this," she whispers. "I can't think when I feel your hands on me."

"You're talking right now, Petal." I circle the pad of my finger over her clit again, and again, slowly because I know it's driving her mad.

"Eat my pussy," she blurts out. "Will you?"

Fuck. Me.

I oblige because the woman I love wants something I crave like a starving man. I push her on her back, slide down and lower my mouth to her clit.

She bucks under me, her fingernails digging into my scalp, words that make no sense spilling from her mouth.

I lick, suck and finger this sweetness until I feel her body tense, her breathing stutter and she comes against my lips.

***

An hour later, her hand is between my legs. "You know how big this is, right?"

I laugh as I throw my forearm over my face. I should be dead asleep by now. I've been up for almost twenty-four hours, but if I have to walk through the next twenty-four like a motherfucking zombie, I'll do it.

Her pussy is my addiction.

"It's big enough," I quip. "I didn't hear you complain about it the other day when you were coming all over it."

"I don't want anyone else to ever touch it," she whispers into the flesh of my neck.

My heart stutters. I think she's telling me in a round-about, hot-as-fuck way that she's in love with me too. Naturally, I can't think of the right thing to say, so I blurt out what's sitting on the edge of my tongue. "Sometimes I like to touch it."

"Oh God," she moans. "Can I watch you do that?"

Well, fuck.

In the space of ten seconds, I shut down a semi-romantic, almost life changing moment and replaced it with an invitation to watch me jerk-off.

I peek at her from behind my arm. "Only if you let me watch you."

"Touch myself?"

"No, bake a fucking cake, Petal." I shake my head. "Yes. I want to watch you finger that hot little pussy of yours."

"Your mouth is so dirty." She squirms next to me. "I like that."

"You fucking love it." I smile my best dimpled grin. "Lay on your back and touch yourself. I'll stand over you and stroke this monster."

She draws in a heavy breath. "Have you done that with a woman before, Smith?"

Of course, I have. I've done everything, sometimes twice on Sundays. I'm no saint. For the most part, she is, so I'm keeping my experience locked down.

"I touch myself when I think about you," I answer as diplomatically as I can.

"Really?" She rolls onto her back, her fingers skimming over her nipples.

I move to straddle her, my knees on either side of hers. I touch the head of my cock, short, easy strokes. "All the damn time. The first day I saw you at the gym, I came thinking about you."

"You screwed that Caprice girl that day."

With my eyes shut and my mind on one woman, and one woman only. I admit, I fucked Caprice that afternoon with Brynn on my brain. I'm not proud of it.

"I left her place, came here and shot a load all over the sheets of this bed thinking about you."

I did. I have no idea where I got the energy to make that happen, but it felt like heaven.

Her hands roam over her thighs. She circles them both before her fingers dip between them. Her lips part slightly and a faint moan escapes.

"Did you touch yourself thinking about me, Petal, or was I still on your man-I-hate-more-than-anything list?"

"My friend, Adley, told me to hate-fuck you."

"I like this Adley person."

She laughs. It's husky and smooth. "She said she could tell I wanted you. She was right. I did."

I slide my hand over the length of my dick. I'm not going to come like this. I want to be inside of her when that happens.

"You should have done it." I groan as I see the wetness from her pussy glistening on her fingers.

"If I walked up to you," she says before her voice trails as her fingers move faster. "If I walked up to you in the gym and told you I wanted to sleep with you, what would you have done?"

"This." I move quickly, pushing her knees apart, settling between them. I run my tongue over the pulse in her neck and my cock over her throbbing clit. "Use my dick to get yourself off. Rub it against your clit."

She shakes her head. "Just fuck me now. I trust you."

"I'm clean," I hiss as I cup her ass and slide into her with my cock bare, beautifully bare.

Chapter 23

Smith

"You haven't said a damn word." I walk up behind her and rest my hands on her shoulders. She's wearing a royal blue, off –the-shoulder, dress today. Her hair is tied into a high ponytail and her face is freshly washed.

I should know. I blew my load all over her mouth and onto her tongue an hour ago in the shower at my place after we got back from the gym. I returned the favor and licked her to an orgasm before we both got dressed to head here.

"I think this place is magnificent." Her eyes travel over the details on the ceiling. "You can't recreate something like this, Smith. I'm telling you this is a rare jewel."

I'd agree if she were talking about herself. Brynn is my jewel. She's the brightest light I've ever seen. Over the past month, she's worked hard on finishing up the bedroom for the Pentlows and now that they've offered her the rest of the apartment to redesign, she's on cloud nine. She's also putting her all into the show suite at The Beryl. She's not happy with how she landed that gig, but she's determined to prove that she's worthy of it.

I've listened to her talk non-stop about her plans for this place. It's the brownstone in Brooklyn that I'm fixing up for my sister and her kids.

"Your designer's touch is going to bring this place back to life." I kiss her softly on the back of her neck. "I love the ideas you have for the boys' rooms. They're going to lose it, Petal. Once they walk in and see what you've done, I swear to fuck they're going to lose it."

She spins around and smiles up at me. "I want this to be a home, a real home that they can grow in and build memories in. Just like Simon's family is doing on the Upper East Side."

We've been over to Simon's place twice this past month for dinner. My family loves this woman. They can't get enough of her. I can't blame them for that. I feel the very same way about her.

"It'll be the perfect home for them." I glance over at the red brick fireplace. "I think we should paint the fireplace white, and add a mantel made of reclaimed wood."

Her brows peak. "Oh is that so? You can't call yourself an expert just because video clips of you hammering a nail into a piece of wood have gone viral."

"There are so many dirty things I can say in response to that." I skim a finger over her now-hardened nipple. "I'll refrain until we're back at my place."

"I wish they would have called the segment something other than *Smith's Sweat Equity*."

That was the brainchild of Resa. She's the one who dubbed my once-a-week segment on Rise and Shine with that name. It's not original, it doesn't slide off the tongue, but it does capture the essence of what I'm doing.

We had no idea how popular those ten-minute segments would become. They've racked up millions of views online in just a few short weeks.

I don't give a shit about any of that. I work here as often as I can, tearing down walls, building new ones and eating dinner with my love on the workbench we've christened our new dining room table.

I'm creating a home for my sister with my own hands. I did the same for my brother. I take care of my own. It's part of the fabric of who I am.

I'm thankful as fuck that part of my deal with taking this on Rise and Shine is that they are footing half the bill for the contractors I've hired. I do as much of the work as I can, but I'm not a professional. I'm just a guy who loves working with his hands so he can give the people he loves a better life.

"What would you have called it?" I ask with a sly grin. "*Smith's Hard Body? Smith's Hands Can Handle It? Smith and His Huge Hammer?*"

"Save those for our private sex tapes." She runs her hands down the front of my blue button down shirt.

"We're making a sex tape?" I unbuckle my belt. "I think we need to rehearse for that."

"Here?" Her eyes scan the floor and the pile of drop cloths I threw in the corner for when I finally get to the painting stage.

"Let me set the scene." I tug her dress down until her perfectly round tits pop out. "I suck on these beauties first."

I lower my mouth to her left breast and slowly draw her pebbled nipple between my teeth.

She hisses at the sensation. "Go on."

I yank the dress down in one fluid movement until it's puddled around her sandaled feet. "Then I lick a path all the way to the most perfect pussy in the world."

Her hands tangle in my hair as I sweep my tongue over her smooth, soft stomach while I slide her blue lace panties off.

"Get to the part where there's actual fucking."

I smile against her tender flesh. "Your wish is my command, you impatient little Petal."

I stand, lift my chin in silence to motion her to take a step back and then another and as she does, I lose every piece of my clothing until she's on her back on the drop cloths, her legs wrapped around me.

"Don't ask me if this has a happy ending." I slide my dick inside her lush, beautiful body.

"It does." She moans as she claws at my arms. "He loves her and she…"

Fuck my dick. It always interrupts her right when she's about to tell me she loves me. I pump hard, so fucking hard. I want to screw those three words out of her. I want to hear them. I need to.

"He loves her," I say through clenched teeth." And she…"

Her back arches as she chases her first release of the afternoon. "She loves him, oh fuck, does she ever love him."

Epilogue

6 Months Later

Brynn

"Who is she?" I brush my fingers over my brother's shoulder. He's wearing a tuxedo and a look on his face I've never seen before.

"Who?" He turns toward me. "You look beautiful, Brynn. Stunning."

I know I do. I chose this particular dress over a month ago. It's short, fitted and black, as required by the black tie affair my brother is hosting to launch his first ever residence hotel in New York. We're in the main ballroom as he oversees a party attended by top notch real estate agents and their clients who have money to burn.

You'd think that managing the construction of the hotel in Paris at the same time would be too much, but he's on top of every detail, including my touches on the residences here in New York. I was thrilled when he hired me for the job.

"You look good too, Julian." I tilt my chin to the opposite side of the room. "I was asking about the pretty woman wearing the stunning diamond earrings. She's standing next to the man in the dark rimmed eyeglasses."

He looks in their direction, his gaze lingering a moment too long. "That's Maya Baker. She's a broker."

"Does she work for dad?"

He finally tears himself away from her to look back at me. "No. Can I get you a glass of champagne?"

"No champagne for me. How do you know her?" I push because I've never seen Julian so flustered. He's always the one who is in complete control. Yet, right now, perspiration is dotting his upper lip and his hand is fisted so tightly around the tumbler of scotch he's holding that I'm certain it's going to shatter into a million pieces at our feet.

He takes a drink from the glass. "Why all the questions?"

"I want you to be as happy as I am." I glance over to where Smith is deep in conversation with two men. "I love you and I want that for you."

"I love you too." He leans forward to brush his lips against my cheek. "I am happy."

"Does Isadora make your heart pound the way it does when you look at Maya?"

"My heart isn't pounding, Brynn."

I glance at his neck and the vein that's visible over the collar of his starched white dress shirt. "Don't lie to yourself, Julian. You don't have to stay with Isadora forever."

"I care for her."

"I'm crazy in love with Smith," I counter. "I race home from work every day, so I can see him. I can't imagine a day without kissing him. He's in my heart, Julian. I can feel him in there with every beat it takes."

He glances back at Maya. "I'm happy for both of you."

I exhale harshly. "I trust you to know what's best for you. I'm always around if you want to talk to me, you know that, don't you?"

"I'm here for you too." He squeezes my hand. "When are you going to make an honest man out of Smith?"

I'm wondering the same thing myself. We've taken every step but the one where my great-grandmother's ring lands on my finger. Pike and I moved in with Smith four months ago. I put my place up for sale and helped Sydney move her stuff into the extra bedroom at Adley's apartment. They hit it off immediately and now when I go see one of my best friends, I get to see them both at the same time.

"I have a surprise for him tonight."

He eyes my face. "Whatever it is, he's going to love it. He's a good man, Brynn. The best man I know."

He is. He's helped me immensely these past few months. He's gone to therapy with me so I can finally let go of the grief and anger that has haunted me since my grandma died.

Smith's been by my side as I've reconnected with my family. He's gone to Sunday dinners at my parents' apartment with me and held my hand while I made small talk with my dad.

Things are in a better place with Fulton and me now. We lunch together every second Wednesday at a deli we used to go to when I was a little girl. He leaves his phone at his office and focuses every ounce of his attention on me.

We have a long road to get things to where we want them to be, but we're moving forward.

"Did he tell you that he got a tattoo?" I ask, proud of the fact that Smith chose to a get a tattoo on the left side of his chest that matches the one on my elbow. It's a simple heart with the word *family* written inside of it.

I took inspiration for mine from a drawing my grandma did inside the birthday card she gave me when I was fourteen. Smith took inspiration for his from my tattoo.

Julian laughs. "Smith? He did that? Tattoos hurt like hell. I didn't think he had it in him."

"How would you know how much tattoos hurt?"

He shoots me a look. "That's none of your business."

I giggle as I kiss his cheek. "You're a tough one to figure out. I like that about you."

***

"Were you and your brother plotting the takeover of more of Manhattan's real estate?" Smith pulls me into a quiet corner of the now crowded room. "I was admiring you from afar when you were talking to him. Jesus, woman, your body is killer in that dress."

"You like?" I spin around so he can catch of glimpse of me from all angles.

"I love." He tugs me into his chest. "I want to go home."

"You have tomorrow off." I look down at the silver watch on my wrist. "No early beddy-bye time for my man tonight. You'll enjoy yourself at this party and then I'll blow you on the ride home in the backseat of the car."

He glances down at the front of his tuxedo pants. "Thanks for that. My cock is at full attention now."

"My brother owns this hotel. I bet I can get us a good hourly rate on a room."

"Hourly rate?" He buries his face in my hair, his lips brushing over the shell of my ear. "Once I get you out of that dress, it's going to be hours until you leave my arms."

"We'll stay for another thirty minutes and then we can leave," I promise with a pat to his cheek. "I have a surprise for you tonight."

"For me?" He questions roughly. "I'm the most impatient man on earth when it comes to you. Tell me what it is now."

"No." I kiss him hard on the mouth. "You have to wait."

I watch him twist his lips as he thinks about it. "I have a surprise for you too, Brynn. I can give it to you now."

"You say the same thing to me every morning," I deadpan. "It's not a surprise anymore, Smith. I know it's your cock and no, you can't give it to me now."

"It's this." He drops to one knee.

What the hell? He drops to one knee and pulls my great-grandma's ring from his pocket.

I knew he had it. I noticed it missing last week.

"All I want in this life is you." He looks up and into my eyes. "You are my sunshine. You give me hope. You're the most incredible person that has ever walked the face of this earth and I promise you that if you will be my wife, I will treasure you every single day until I die in your arms because there's no way in hell I'll spend one moment without you."

"Smith," I breathe out his name slowly. "Oh my God."

"Marry me on the rooftop at the top of the world, my beautiful Petal. Let me show you every day how much I love you."

I cover my hand with my mouth knowing that I'm about to scream out in pure joy. This day started out in the most amazing way possible and now it's ending with a proposal from the man I love more than life itself.

"Say yes," he urges. "Please say yes."

I pull him up with both hands by the lapel of his jacket. "Let me give you my surprise first."

His smile fades. "Why? I need you to say yes. I'm dying here."

I reach in my clutch and pull out a small white rectangular box. I wrapped a red ribbon around it this morning. My hands were shaking, tears were streaming down my face and as I watched Smith on Rise and Shine on the television in our apartment, I felt my heart burst wide open.

"Open it." I push it at him. "Just open it."

He nods in silence.

It feels like eternity as he slowly unties the ribbon and removes the lid of the box. His hands fumble with the white tissue paper before they still.

"Brynn."

Just my name comes from his lips and then tears stream down his cheeks.

"I don't know what the hell this means but I know what I want it to mean."

I touch the tip of the test stick. "Two lines means yes. Yes, I'll marry you and yes, we're having a baby."

He pulls me to him, cradling the back of my head in his hand. "We are leaving now. I need to make love to my fiancée. I may need to cry too, but they're happy tears, Petal. The happiest tears I've ever cried."

I pull back and look up into the face of the man I've been destined to love since I was seventeen. "We're the luckiest, Smith. You and I are the luckiest."

"Life can't get much better than this." He smiles and those damn dimples weaken my knees.

"It will." I perch on my tiptoes to kiss his mouth. "Every day of this life we're building together will be better than the last. I can't wait to see what the future has in store for us."

Preview of Troublemaker

Crew

There are certain luxuries afforded a man when he owns a club in Manhattan. He can drink the best scotch in the world and expense that shit. He can pick a different woman every night of the week and he can sit on his ass and watch one of his best friends get hit on by some schmuck in a suit that's two sizes too big or he can do something about it.

I've had my fill of scotch tonight and the woman I was with last night is waiting for me back at her place. I can't leave my club, Veil East, yet. That's because, Adley York, one of my closest friends is about to go home with a professional baseball player with a reputation for hitting it out of the park.

It shouldn't matter to me if another man is stellar in bed. I don't compare myself to anyone. I've never had a complaint in all the years I've been active on the Manhattan social scene. I have zero doubt that I've fucked more women than Trey Hale, but by the look of what's happening on the dance floor, he's about to take Adley home to screw her.

That is not happening on my watch.

I can't have her because there are women that you friend and women that you fuck. Adley falls squarely in the first category although my traitorous cock wants her in the second. It can't happen. If I take that petite blond to bed, I'll lose her and the hole that would leave in my life is something I don't have the fucking emotional maturity to deal with.

"Adley," I call out her name over the booming beat that vibrates off the walls. Why the hell did I have a state of the art sound system installed in this place? "Hey, Ad."

By the grace of God, she notices me pointing at her. She tosses me a wave and a wiggle of her ass before she grabs hold of the star pitcher's shoulders. I swear to fuck if she climbs up on that right now, I'll haul her off the floor over my shoulder.

I motion for her to come to where I'm standing. Shaking her head, she flips me the bird.

I slam my now empty tumbler on the bar and stalk toward her.

"I need to talk to you." I stand next to her. "It's important, Adley."

"It can wait, Crew." Her pretty face flushes. "I'm a little busy right now."

She's a little drunk right now. I see it in her eyes and her hips. She's aching for some and if anyone is going to give it to her, it'll be me.

No. I fucking can't. Those perfect tits and that curvy ass are off-limits.

"I'm going to drop you off at your apartment." I take a quick look around. The club is running smoothly tonight. We're at full capacity. I don't need to be here to benefit from this. "Grab your stuff and let's go."

"Why would l do that?" Her eyes rake my six-foot –three, two-hundred-pound frame. The fact that my black button down shirt, matching pants and shoes are all designer labels doesn't impress Adley. It never has. "You're not as fun as Trey is."

Trey has nothing on me. I'm taller, richer, and a hell of a lot better looking than he is. I own a mirror. Black hair, green eyes and a smile that has never failed me to date are what I see every morning.

"You've had too much to drink, Ad."

"Maybe you haven't had enough." She pokes her finger into the center my chest. "You work out."

Like a madman, every morning at five a.m. before the city wakes up. "We're leaving."

"What if I want to go with him?"

"Pick another night to make that happen." I direct that statement to Hale. "She's not going anywhere with you tonight."

"Who are you? Her husband?"

Adley laughs so hard she bends over revealing a perfect bird's eye view of the top of her round breasts. The decent thing to do is to look away, but I don't.

"I'm her friend. I own the club." I push a hand at him. "Crew Benton."

"You're Benton?" He steps closer and studies my face, his hand eagerly shaking mine. "Your reputation precedes you, man."

I have no idea what the fuck that means, so I steer him to a place I'll know he'll go. "Your drinks are on the house for the rest of the night. Tell Penny at the bar, Crew's got the tab."

"No shit?"

"No shit," I repeat back. "It's a limited time offer so..."

"Understood." He doesn't give Adley another look before he heads for the bar.

"That was a cock-block, a totally intentional cock-block." She frowns. "You ruined my night. Now, what am I supposed to do?"

I eye her up. Small black dress, hair so messed up that she looks like she just fucked in the back of a beat-up pickup truck and a mouth that was made for sin. "Come to my place, Adley. I want you to come home with me."

Coming soon

Preview of WORTH

A Two-Part Novel Duet

I notice him immediately. It's impossible not to. Julian Bishop is the man of the hour, after all. This celebration, complete with expensive champagne and stiff-backed wait staff, has drawn the crème de la crème of Manhattan's social elite. It's the place to be tonight, and with a lot of crafty manipulation and a fair bit of luck, I'm standing in the midst of it, wearing a killer little black dress and diamond earrings I borrowed from a broker who has sold more than her fair share of apartments with Park Avenue addresses.

"I got you another glass of champagne, Maya."

I turn toward my date for the evening, taking the tall crystal flute from his hand. I enjoy a small sip while I look at his hands. They're adequate, not too large, and not too small. Those hands, along with the brief kiss he gave me when he picked me up tonight promise a night of passion that would be forgettable at best. He's nothing to write home about or to write about at all, for that matter.

"Thanks, Charlie," I purr. "Where's your drink?"

He nudges the sexy-as-all-hell, black-rimmed glasses up his nose with his index finger. He has a nerd with a side of male model look. That's what made me stop at his desk two weeks ago to ask if I could borrow his stapler.

I don't staple. If I did, I'm sure I'd find one in my desk, hidden underneath the three dresses and two pairs of shoes I have tucked in the drawer. I never know when a change of wardrobe is called for. A girl has to be ready for anything when she's trying to claw her way up the hierarchy of the Manhattan real estate market.

"I had one. That's my limit." He squints as he looks at the bar. "Is she here yet? I heard someone say she's going to make an entrance."

I heard someone say she's a dirty, dirty slut.

That someone was me. I said it to myself. She's far from dirty or slutty. She's a lawyer, Harvard educated, with looks to rival her brains. Jealousy is a filthy accessory and I don't wear it well at all.

"I don't think she's arrived." I turn back to where Julian's standing. He looks identical to the way he did when I first laid eyes on him. That was more than a year ago. I was helping a friend and he was offering her a job. Our paths crossed, the energy flowed and then he left. I never saw the man again.

I would have settled for one tumble in the sheets of his bed. A brief encounter would have satisfied my craving but it wasn't meant to be. He continued on his happily-ever-path and I swam the dating waters of Manhattan occasionally snagging a Charlie in my net.

"I'm going to mingle," I say it like I mean it. "I'll meet you back here in thirty."

Charlie looks down at his watch. It's not impressive. That's not Charlie's style.

"Thirty minutes, Maya." He touches the lenses of his glasses with two of his fingers before he points them right at me. "I'm going to have my eye on you."

Good for you, Cowboy.

I take my champagne, my spirit of adventure and my too tight black heels and I walk across the room. I took my time getting dressed tonight just for that one split second that we all live for. It's that moment when the man you imagine running naked through a field of daisies with or fucking in a back alley, turns and looks at you.

I've been planning this for two months.

Plotting every word I'll say when his eyes meet mine. I'm counting on him remembering me because I've been told I'm not easy to forget.

"Maya Baker." The voice behind me is unmistakably his. Warm with a hint of control, deep with a promise of pleasure.

I start to pivot at the sound of it. It's a beacon, a pull that is too strong to resist.

"Don't turn around." A hand, steady and determined, rests on my hip. The fingertips assert enough pressure to control my movement. "I don't recall seeing your name on the guest list."

Something's caught Julian's cock's attention. I can feel it pressing against me in the middle of this crowded room while we wait for his business partner, rumored lover and person I'd most like to lock in a closet for eternity to arrive. "I was a last minute addition."

"A welcome addition," he adds. "Are you enjoying yourself?"

I feel the undercurrent of desire. It was there last year when we met. It's stronger now.

"I am now." I push my fingers into his on my hip.

His chest lifts and falls. "I'm needed on the stage. You won't run away before we have a chance to talk, will you?"

I turn my head to look up at him. Black hair, ocean blue eyes and a face that would make any woman lock her office door to imagine a moment alone with him.

I've done it. Many women in Manhattan have.

"You're as handsome as ever, Julian."

He rounds me, his hand still holding mine. "You're more enchanting than the day we met, Maya. I've followed your career. I have a position I think you'd be interested in."

Coming soon

THANK YOU

Thank you for purchasing my book. I can't even begin to put to words what it means to me. If you enjoyed it, please remember to write a review for it. Let me know your thoughts! I want to keep my readers happy.

For more information on new series and standalones, please visit my website, www.deborahbladon.com. There are book trailers and other goodies to check out.

If you want to chat with me personally, please LIKE my page on Facebook. I love connecting with all of my readers because without you, none of this would be possible.
www.facebook.com/authordeborahbladon

Thank you, for everything.

ABOUT THE AUTHOR

Deborah Bladon has never read a romance hero she didn't like. Her love for romance novels began when she was old enough to board the bus, library card in hand to check out the newest Harlequin paperbacks. She's a Canadian by heart, and by passport, but you can often spot her in New York City sipping a latte and looking for inspiration for her next story. Manhattan is definitely her second home.

She cherishes her family and believes that each day is a gift for writing, for reading, and for loving.

Made in the USA
Lexington, KY
02 May 2018